Second Rising

To Gareth—
I hope you enjoy!
Best,
Catherine

Second Rising

A NOVEL

CATHERINE M.A. WIEBE

Blue Butterfly Books

THINK FREE, BE FREE

Blue Butterfly Book Publishing Inc.
2583 Lakeshore Boulevard West
Toronto, Ontario, Canada M8V 1G3
Tel 416-255-3930 Fax 416-252-8291
Ordering information: www.bluebutterflybooks.ca

First edition, soft cover: 2009

Library and Archives Canada Cataloguing in Publication

Wiebe, Catherine M.A. (Catherine Marion Abbott), 1984–
Second rising : a novel

ISBN 978-0-9784982-4-5

I. Title.

PS8645.I32S42 2008 C813'.6 C2008-906787-8

Design and typesetting by Fox Meadow Creations
Text set in Fairfield Light
Printed in Canada by Transcontinental-Métrolitho
Forest-friendly paper (100% post-consumer recycled fibre)

No government grants were sought nor any public subsidies received for publication of this book. Blue Butterfly Books thanks book buyers for their support in the marketplace.

To my grandmothers,

Marion Madeline Abbott

and

Mary Wiebe

Was it important, anymore, to remember?

Or is memory just the vanity of the forgotten, all our love for memory only a desire to be remembered?

one

How do you describe the time before words?

How do you create flesh from water and salt, pry open hands holding nothing and wrap them around your own? Dissolve food in milky water and pour memory into mouths unaccustomed to eating?

We use pictures for words and food for memory. You will not remember this unless there is a photograph, so let me take one now, and now, and now. Sit here where you never sit and hold her like you will not again, and this can be your memory. Eat this dish that I made for you, and these apples, the first of the season, that will not come again until she is older (when you will pick them together, she slung across your back).

Eat this, and this, and these. There are no words, yet, and the pictures are stored inside this box, so you should sleep and remember, sleep and forget—for sleep, too, will not come again until she is older. (And when it comes, it will be the sleep of mothers and of their mothers before them, sleep crossed with memories of childhood and apprehensions of old age.)

So sleep and remember, remember in the place where you do not need words to do so.

❧

How do you describe the time before sound?

How do you make souls from the beating

of air, count time with hearts still inseparable from feet?

We use pictures for sounds, trace with our feet and our fingers the shape of the silence grown louder. You will not remember this unless you know to make it remembered, so hold this and breathe in and do not whisper your doubts because she can hear you.

Before there is sound there are memories of sounds, and the shape of your words in her dreams.

❧

How do you describe a time before space?

Where does this piece go, and this one; where do we keep this thought, and this one, and this one? How do you make fullness from nothing, push two dimensions into three?

You cannot know without numbers to tell you, so hold this and stay still and wait while I wrap this around you. Here there will be food, and here will be memory, and here, in this space between them, is where her heart goes. You will make a space for her, don't worry.

Before and behind you are spaces to steal from, someone else will be empty so that you can be full; someone else will breathe out so that you can inhale. You will find a space for her, don't worry.

ꕥ

You were born with a hole in your heart, said my grandmother. Each of us is born with a hole in our heart, between the memory of things past and the memory of things to come.

It has closed, already, she said, it closed before you remembered anything, because you do not remember until it is closed, until the part of you that still wishes not to be born is sealed up inside your heart, alone with its beating silence and salty breaths. When it is closed, you have lost your memories of the time before birth, and begun your memories of life.

(And when I say lost, I mean, as we usually mean, forgotten.)

Memories are not new, they are never new, she continued. You do not build your memory from nothing, placing great stones in the formless deep, covering the emptiness that was there. Memories are paper, paste and glue, bread crusts soaked and stuffed in the cracks and spread over the faces of other memories we now call forgotten.

They are seals against the time before birth, against the memories of water and salt that leak out from the hole in your heart and dissolve the memories of this life, of paper and bread and muddy paste. For some, the hole is never closed, is left unsealed; they are always forgetting, even when they are young, always confusing memory with truth and what is passing with what once was or will be. For some, the hole opens again, in a burst like water breaking or slowly in a hundred tiny leaks. The seal is broken and your memories dissolved, the newest, wettest ones first, and the older ones resisting, for a time. For some, the hole closes just as they are born, and is never open again.

You must pray that the hole in your heart is closed, that it will never open, that you will forget the words I have said to you. Forget so that you may remember.

Food grows in your belly, that is how you remember, she said.

You were empty when you were born, perfect and dead inside. Nothing grew in your belly then. And still nothing grew after you were born, and suckled by your mother, who turned herself inside out again, and again, to feed you on the taste of what was before, on the milk of forgetting. So it is that we cannot remember new things, even after we are born.

Your mother has told you, perhaps, that you must eat to live? That you must have bread and vegetables in equal proportion inside you, and meat in the space in between them? You must eat to live, it is true. But you also must eat to remember, because memory grows in the pit of your stomach, from things killed, eaten, and born again. Food grows into memory, and memory will sustain you.

You do not remember when you were born, she continued, raising her voice at the end to ask the question whose answer she knew. Nor after you were born nor before. Because your mother's milk is only the memory of what was before, the memory of being inside, of being home before you knew what home was. So it is that you cannot remember the new things, even after you are born.

And so we will remember for you, we who are old and whose insides are growing though our outsides have stopped, we who are shrinking, whose memories live in our bellies. We will remember for you, chew and digest your first days, and feed them back to you when you are older.

We will remember for you, so sleep and forget.

We will remember for you, until your belly is full of food and your memories grow inside you, until we no longer need to tend to you, and you instead are tending to us.

17

You do not remember when you were born, my grandmother said. You do not remember what it is to be alive and not yet born; you do not know, any more, where you have come from.

You know only where you are, and even that imperfectly.

You were born in the fall, on the edge of summer, when the trees are turning colour but have not yet turned in on themselves, on a great, rich, velvety day. I was born in the fall, on the edge of winter, in the time when the leaves are dead and the days are hard, made from twigs fallen down and gathered into bundles for burning. Your sister was born in the summer, on a hot, wet day, with air made from the dripping juice of pink peaches.

We were each born with a hole in our hearts.

My grandmother had a sister, my great-aunt Marguerite. She died before I was born, just after my mother learned to remember.

She was born with a hole in her heart, my mother says, when I ask her why she died. She was born with a hole in her heart, and there was nothing they could do for her. Nowadays they can fix it, make new hearts and new walls between what was and what is. But they couldn't do anything for her then; her heart was unravelling, the hole getting bigger until it was more hole than heart, and she died. She was born with a hole in her heart, my mother says again.

You already said that part, I said, you already said it twice.

We are each born with a hole in our hearts, replies my grandmother, when I ask her about what my mother said. Your mother understands much more than she lets on, though less than she pretends to. But now is not the time to talk of that. Now I will tell you a story of the time before you were born.

Your mother burst out from herself suddenly, with the tulips; they came later then than they do now. All of spring came later, then; it was shorter, sweet like the first asparagus. Your mother was late, too, her belly held flat for far too long.

But then the bits of green, the beginnings of crocuses, were there, and now you cannot make yourself remember what the ground looked like without them, or even that the ground was without them yesterday, or a few days past. And her belly burst out, a sudden sponge of dough, kneading itself from within and rising with the heat of the day. And so it is how it is, and we do not remember how it was before.

You were the happiest moment of the spring, she said, though you were not yet born and cannot remember how happy we were, how we could no longer imagine what it was to be sad. You pushed out her belly and gave her a space for food again, and I made all of her favourite dishes when she came to visit.

She came to stay that spring, pushed your father out the door to his exhibition, though he did not want to leave her. She took him to the train and then came here, to stay in her old bedroom. Your grandfather was gone at first, so it was just the two of us in this old house, eating and laughing and eating and laughing some more.

We made bread that week, loaves and rolls and cornbread and muffins; we made a different kind nearly every day, took it to the neighbours, and then to friends the next road over, and left some out for the hired man to take home, and still there was enough for us to eat and eat. Your mother grew fat with bread that spring, or fat with you, or both.

She was beautiful and round, and we set the bread to rise by her belly.

Oh, still not as big as my little one, she would say (for we did not yet know your name)—we had better leave it a little while longer, maybe another chapter or another hand of cards?

Another hand of cards and another loaf of bread and soon, too soon, your grandfather was home. And soon, not soon enough, your father was returned from his show. He had sold a painting; we made bread to celebrate, and that was the spring we all forgot how to be sad.

I had forgotten, too, how it is to be with child in the summer. Your mother grew larger and larger, her ankles swelled and then her knees and then her wrists—this child is making new spaces inside me, she laughed. And I pictured you, tiny and stretching down, pushing now around her left knee, now around her right, smoothing and shaping, a potter working from inside her vessel.

And then you were born, as summer tipped over into fall.

❧

You were born with a hole in your heart,

Put the bread in here, and the paste and the dirt. Mix them together—use this spoon or your hands.

between the memory of things past and things still to come.

Spread it here, in the spaces between the ribs; push it in to the cracks to fill them.

You cannot remember until it is closed,

We are making a new heart—

until the hole is sealed against forgetting.

a heart with no memory of the time before birth;

So you must close it, now, before it grows bigger.

a heart that cannot forget the things of this life.

Take this bread, it is still warm from the oven, push it into the cracks to fill them.

Put it here, in the oven, to dry. Here, where it is still warm from the bread.

❧

Birth tastes like white things—snow and milk and the centres of bread. New things that are actually old, refashioned from rivers and grass and the yeast that lives in the air.

Your mother turned herself inside out to bear you, and then again (and again) in smaller ways to feed you, first on milk and then on the centres of fruits, over-ripened and soft. You will long for those days, one day, though you cannot imagine it now.

I taste of white things, too, though I am far from being born; age tastes of white things, of old things no longer playing at being new.

Between birth and old age there is youth and the memory of it, and the taste of white things grows faint. But then it grows stronger again, and you will think that your youth has returned, though you will be wrong. You will stretch out your hands to receive it, but they will close instead around the indignities of childhood. You will be fed once more on bread soaked in milk and the memories of others, your memories held in trust to be disbursed once you come of age.

(Dying too, tastes of white things, of stale bread and ashes pushed down the throats of those who can no longer refuse them. But now is not the time to talk of that.)

❧

When you are born, you see with your skin.

There is flesh instead of sight, skin instead of hearing. There is flesh circumscribed by other flesh in widening circles, passed between hands—soft, warm, paper, silk, hair, cold, bumpy, hot. Passed between hands and pressed into faces you will not remember. Memories are soft, now, and easily altered, close to the surface and fragile.

Later, you will remember the skin, its smell and the taste it left behind on your hands, the smells on your clothes. Your memory is in your skin, at first. You memorize by touch, by taste, cataloguing other flesh—soft, warm, paper, silk, hair, cold, bumpy, hot. Salt, sweet, grit, bitter, smooth. To know is to touch and to taste. To remember is to taste again.

You will remember with your skin again, when you are older. To know is to touch, to taste, to be fooled by touch and taste into memories not your own. To remember is to taste again. Your oldest memories, your first memories, are in your skin, and your youngest ones—the last ones—are there, too.

Memories are brittle, then, and easily broken; paper skin with straw veins, close to the surface and fragile. Easily fooled, too, by bowls of soup and the hands of one who is not your child, stroking your forehead and telling you to rest, rest.

But now you remember with your skin and later you will remember with your mind and your slips of paper and your numbers that tell you where to find things. And later still, you will remember with your skin again, fooling yourself (or wanting to be fooled) by children not your own, holding bowls of soup and bread they did not make.

But now you remember with your skin, said my grandmother. She was talking to my sister, soon after she was born, or she was talking to another baby, the child of the neighbour. Or she was talking to me and there is a photograph of her talking to me, so I think I remember, when really I have only heard her tell me what she said before.

She lets me hold her wrist, with its dangling skin in place of bracelets, in both my hands and twist it until it hurts. I can twist her skin much further than she can twist mine, because hers is baggy and does not hurt so much as mine, which is stretched tight and can hardly be twisted at all before it burns.

Your skin will not always fit so perfectly, she says. When you are old, it will sag with the weight of your memory, thoughts that used to be in your mind will seep out through your skin. You will try to catch them as they drip away, making memories from paper and photographs, re-sticking them to the walls of your mind. You will tell stories to others for the benefit of yourself, sure that this telling will make it stay, will make it brighter instead of faint.

And at that time, you will eat not to remember, or to be remembered, but only to fill up the spaces inside your skin, to make it fit again instead of looking like the flesh-dress of someone twice your size.

I am twisting the skin of her arm all this time, twisting and wondering why it is brown and bumpy in spots and cool like the paper my mother keeps in the tray in the shade of her desk. She is stretched out (or her skin is), bowed like a clothesline with too many pants strung on. I let go of her wrist and pull the skin out from it at different angles, judging the extra and seeing what I could fit inside to make it fluff out, to make it more like mine.

In her skin are memories tired of sharing space with others, memories that sag away from her bones, trying to make new spaces for themselves, trying to distinguish themselves again. They are threadbare from too many retellings, washed together and jumbled up with others so that it is impossible to tell from the grey rags bumping around whether this one was once red or green or blue or striped or plain.

ℬ

Thursday is wash day, and the clothes are sorted into piles. The water is white and bubbly and warm, like a bath. My grandmother peels off her skin—it frightens me, though I have seen it before—and throws it into the wash.

How do you know that it won't wash away? I ask.

She doesn't answer my question, not quite—the water will shrink it so that it will fit better, she says. The memories inside will be held on tighter; they will not droop away from my bones and become forgotten.

When you are old like me, she continues, you see with your skin again. It is tricky, though, not like when you are younger; your skin is at once absorbing new things and absorbed in not forgetting the old ones. Things leach in and out through your skin. And bits break off, brittle with age and the effort of memory, tired of holding on and happy at the thought of being free again, of being memory unencumbered by flesh (though they do not know that memory without flesh is no memory at all—only, at best, a story).

These are the things my grandmother said to me when I was born, or the things I wish she had said. She pressed her skin into mine, I am certain of that, pressed her face to my belly as she held me above her head and whispered stories that I neither remember nor forget. She pressed her skin to mine, I am certain, pressed her stories into the holes of my skin and my heart.

31

The first word that you knew was your name, said my grandmother. I started to object, but she said no, no, not your first word, as your mother would call it, but the first that you knew. We named you in your time before words, so that when words found you—flew into your ears and around your heart and into your belly and out through your mouth—you would not be unprepared. So that you would greet them as one who is named—as one who claims, already, a word of her own.

You must have a name so that you will remember, so that you will be remembered by others. There is no memory without name. (Or if there is, if some little thought has escaped or been overlooked in the naming of parts, then it is a memory circumscribed, cut off from transmission, because it cannot be told, cannot even be described, except by the baking of bread or the rubbing of salve on a wound. It is qualified, dependant on its container, a memory that fades with the setting of the sun and the shrinking of the mind that holds it.) You must have a name to remember, so we gave you a name in your time before words. You rolled it up in your tongue, and we laughed when you spit it out in different shapes. The first word that you knew was your name.

❧

There were more words, after that, and more stories from the time before my memory begins. Stories, stories, always more stories, my grandmother would say when I asked her what I was like as a child. Always more stories.

❧

Can you read to me?

I was not yet old enough to understand the words in the thick books with letters that sank into the spines with the heaviness of their importance. I was only old enough to understand that they were important, and to imagine that perhaps I, too, would be important if I heard the words inside them.

(I know now that you were not reading to me, that you opened to a page in the middle and then told me stories, that you stayed on one page for hours and hours. I could not find the book to look inside it, but I know that the letters were not small enough for you to stay on one page for so long. (I know, too, that this was always the book that you read from, that you read the same book over and over again, with only the stories different.))

This is the story of where sadness comes from, you said. It is a long story (and here you looked at me over top of the book), and one with many parts. But before I read you the story, we will go and make some soup.

And then I will read to you, when you have soup in your belly and bread in your hands. I will read you the story then. Sadness should never be had on an empty stomach.

I had forgotten this story, the story of the day of soup and sadness, and when it first came to mind, I thought that it took place in the fall. That it was squash soup that we made and bread that was left over from Sunday, steamed to be soft again above the soup. But it was the summer, I remember now, and we made vegetable soup.

I have forgotten the story, though.

❧

Let me remember for you, you said.

I will write your name in black marker on the bottoms of your socks and paste tiny labels in the pocket of your knapsack. This is your name and your address and these are your parents and this is the number to telephone if you need them and you cannot find them. You cannot read the number, but someone else can, and someone else will call for you and place the telephone next to your ear and you will say hello? hello? hello? while it is ringing. And then your mother will say hello? hello? hello, my darling, where are you? Are you alright? And instead of answering, you will just say hello, hello mommy, hello, again and again.

We were out for a walk, the two of us, to the park. You were not really walking, I suppose, I was pushing you or carrying you, or holding your arms above your head while you swung your feet, safe under the arch of my legs. I can see the tag sticking out of your shirt, with your name on it in black marker. It is there in case you forget—your name or your shirt—so that someone else can remember for you.

(I will keep your knowledge safe for you,

on the tags of your shirts and the soles of your shoes, I will put the memories in so many places that you could not possibly forget them. Don't worry, little one, I will be your memory.)

❧

This memory is older than I am—I know because my mother has the same one, she says, from before I was born, when she was the one who helped planting.

We are on our knees in the garden

—bent over in the field, says my mother—

and my grandmother is pulling, from a sack on her shoulder

—a bag at her waist—

the bulbs—some big, as big as my hand in a fist, and some small and beautifully pointed, like cloves of garlic for the garden to eat whole

—the seeds, which are tiny, smaller than the nails on the baby's hands.

She is kneeling, and I am bobbing, up and down, tamping the ground behind her with my rubber boots

—we are drawing lines with our fingers to drop the seeds into—

we are planting a garden for the spring

—food for the summer.

ꕥ

We feasted on tender words.

The only way to finish before dark was to get up in the dark, doing the simplest bits in the grey light before sunrise. We spread out the dish towels (that would be washed and turned into rags after today), put the meat from the butcher's on top of them, and spread more towels on top. Someone else came in to the kitchen, and then someone else—my grandfather? my sister? my mother?—all I remember are hands—and my grandmother passed out the hammer and rolling pin and other things heavy and blunt and good for hitting. We stood in a line at the counter, (with my sister on the floor, I remember now—she was too short to reach to the counter, even with a stool) and began to pound.

I was timid and then suddenly sure, blasting with my rolling pin, making a pockmarked sheet with bits of blood or juice or something squirting out. Enough, enough, my mother said; a bit more, a bit more said my grandmother. More pounding, more squirting, and then—enough, enough, my grandmother said.

She already had the big kitchen scissors in her hand, and she cut the cloth with the meat, and then removed the towels and cut the meat some more, into red and pink ribbons thicker than the ones in my hair. Get the broth on to boil she said to someone, likely my mother. We will be ready soon, and it cannot wait once we are ready. She rolled up her sleeves, and I rolled up mine, staining the cuffs with the blood that I could never avoid getting on my hands. Are you ready? she asked me, smiling, but did not wait for my answer, just handed me the first strip of meat and some thread.

We rolled our memories in flesh and tied them together with thread left over from dresses and quilts. The day was taken by rolling and tying and roasting and simmering, and the smell of new memories turning into old ones filled the kitchen.

You roll them in flesh so they will stick instead of fading, I remember someone saying, and you eat them while they are still warm, while their smell still fills the kitchen, so that they will be both around and inside you, so that you will be submerged in memory, so that you will not forget the taste of this day.

We feasted on tender words as the day grew dark.

two

There was no word in the beginning. Only flesh—soft, still growing, and unruly, like a sponge of dough left too long in a sunny window.

There were no stories, either, only the indentations of the world on flesh, bruises as memories.

There were songs. I remember them without their words; the words came later, when we slept again in my mother's bed and she sang us to sleep with the first songs we knew.

When I was born, my father sang, waiting in the hallway. That was what my grandmother said when I asked what she remembered of my birth. The beginnings are always harder to remember, she says. When things are ending, you know that you're leaving soon, that you must say goodbye. And so you make marks in the spaces, reminders to come back to, decide that the taste of this soup will always be the taste of this moment.

But the beginning is difficult. Either you are too young to remember it, or you don't know that it's happening, or, perhaps worst of all, it is too wrapped up in an ending for you to know that something marvellous is about to start. You get better at seeing beginnings when you are older, she said. But there are fewer of them to be seen.

That is why there are no words for the beginning, why we must invent stories to tell each other where we came from.

&

The first memory I have is not of my grandmother, it is of her food, though perhaps the two are not really different. I was old enough to have memories, but young enough that they had no words assigned to them. My mother added the words later, when we were moving pictures from boxes into albums.

There was a perfect loaf. It was on a plate, silver but made from tin, on the counter between the kitchen and the dining room, which I could only reach from the tall stool that I later remembered for its kick-down footrest. It was sweet loaf, shaped just like the bread in the store, and I knew without cutting it that all the holes inside were perfectly round and white and tiny. There was white icing on top, dripping down the sides, shiny and dull at once, like a frozen pond.

We didn't eat it. Everyone was doing things—getting up from the table, scraping plates, serving coffee, moving around, offering fresh peach pie—but no one was eating the sweet bread with its frozen-pond icing. I picked up the bread and moved it to the small table where I sat for dinners with the whole family, and started to remove the icing. I picked at it until there was nothing left on the bread, and piled it like a snowdrift on the table against the wall. I licked my fingers and rubbed them along the bread, making the brown surface shiny, with all the pores exposed and highlighted, like my mother sunning herself at the beach.

I put it back on the silver-tin plate, and left to play on the velvet flowered couch in the living room. My grandmother told me later that she thought, for a moment, that she had forgotten the icing. But then she saw it, a snowfall on the formica, and realized what I had done. She told me when I was older that she'd never eaten this kind of bread without icing before.

There is sadness inside bread, my grandmother said later. That is what the sweet icing is for, on this one, to cover up the taste of sadness. That is what the butter is for, and the meat and the cheese and the lettuce and pickles and tomatoes on your sandwich. That is why you never see anyone but those men in prison movies eating bread plain, because they are already drowning in sadness so they do not notice the extra taste of it in their bread.

She said she wore perfume for that reason, too—because the sweet smell covered up the sadness inside.

❧

I have an even earlier memory than this one, but it has words attached, so I know that it comes only from photographs.

My grandmother was in the kitchen, making bread. I didn't know what bread was, yet, I hadn't learned about the yeast and the rising and knocking on the top to be sure that nothing was left inside except the sound of the spaces between.

I want to go home, my grandmother tells me I said. It was your first sentence, she said, and already you were leaving. I was playing with a piece of dough in the picture that my mother took from the chair where she sat with her feet up, waiting for my sister to be born. My hair has flour in it, and my grandmother's looks like it does. I know my mother was sitting there because there is a corresponding picture, taken by my grandmother the moment before my mother took hers, of my mother, squinting at us through the camera propped on her belly, smiling with the half of her face that we could see.

❧

My sister was born in the summer.

Once the flour is added, then we knead it.

My father drove my mother to the hospital, and went to park the car.

You are pushing air in with your hands, they are breathing for the dough.

She walked in to the hospital alone, while my father parked the car. In the stickiness of summer it was hard to breathe.

It cannot breathe for itself, but it needs the air to grow. So we push it in. See, see, that is how, you push it in, close it around the air.

She had to sit, waiting, for an hour, which seems longer when you are waiting to fold out onto yourself, like socks after the wash.

You must keep pushing the air in, use the palms of your hands. Here, stand on this stool so you will be a little taller.

My sister was born feet first.

You must turn it inside out, make sure that everything has air, has spaces inside to breathe while we are gone.

The sun was setting when her head came out.

We are almost done, now, put the bowl by the window, in the spot where the sun is still shining.

It was evening when my sister was born.

Set it here to rest, in the bowl by the window, where it is warmest and the sun is still shining.

❧

I stayed with my grandmother while my sister cried. She would say come in, come in, dear one. I have your bed all ready. My father would thank her and leave to go back home.

I didn't know until later that she always had my bed ready, and that she put only chocolates with tight wrappers on the nightstand, so that they would last if I did not come over as soon as she would have liked.

When I stayed with her, she told me about riding the train. My grandmother loved trains, though no one knew that she did.

My grandfather used trains to transport the lumber from his forests to the mills on the island. My father examined them, trying to find out how they worked, wanting to paint their insides. My mother rode them to meetings in the city, when she wrote papers that she gave to people who didn't smile.

My grandmother loved them. She had been on a train once, to the city, before she knew that my grandfather loved her and would name a sawmill for her, in the time when she wanted to be a nurse.

She said that when my sister was old enough, she would take both of us on the train to the city, and that we would eat chocolates directly from the box and not need to put them in a dish as my mother did when we had company.

(When we had company, we had the square chocolates with mint in the middle and the box-ones filled with cherries and raspberry crème. When I found my mother's secret drawer, where she stored the chocolates and the small chocolate dishes for company, I ate them, though they didn't taste as I remembered.)

We would go to the stores, and she would buy for both of us a set of deerskin gloves, which she said would be as soft as my sister's hair after my mother washed it, and as strong as my father when he threw me over his shoulder with one hand and carried me up the stairs to bed. We were only to wear the gloves on Sundays, she said, to church, and also to occasions. When we were in the city, we would finish eating all of the chocolate before we bought our gloves, because it would certainly not behoove us to have stained gloves, she said.

(I spent much time after this conversation picturing my hands turning into hooves if I stained my gloves, and so only wore them inside the car to church on Sundays, taking them off before we left the car to go inside.)

When my sister was a little older, and starting to be quiet at night, my father sang to me instead of taking me to my grandmother's house.

He came to sing after my mother and my sister were in bed, after he thought they might be sleeping. I was the last to fall asleep, or at least the last to stop talking.

My father would come and lie next to me in my bed, and hold my hand, and explain things to me. He explained why engineers on trains were different than engineers in offices, and how escalators worked. He told me about his bachelor days, which was when he used to eat spaghetti out of pots instead of bowls, and mix his vegetables in with his noodles so that he didn't have another dirty dish. He told me that when mum was gone away, we would eat like bachelors.

And then he sang. My father's voice was like wood left out in the rain. He sang hymns, mostly—they were the only music he really knew, I found out later. He did not play music in competitions when he was younger, like my mother did. He didn't have a radio, either, until he met my mother and wanted to get one so that she would be happy. He only heard music in church and from his mother, singing when she thought that no one was listening.

When he sang, and when he explained things, he held my hand. He would squeeze it, while he was singing. If I squeezed back, it meant that I was still awake, and that he should keep singing. If I didn't, it meant that I was asleep and that he could leave—but quietly, or else I would wake up and we would begin again.

My grandmother sang to me too.

She sang to me before my father, after the stories of trains and before I fell asleep, while I sucked on the chocolates that she left beside my bed, but I remember my father's singing more. Perhaps because I was still thinking only of the train and the chocolates out of boxes when she sang, perhaps because I remember all of her food more than any of her singing. Her songs were not like my father's—hymns that our church had already forgotten, sung low so as not to wake up my sister in the next room. My father's songs were for falling asleep, and my grandmother's songs were for dreams.

She sang to me when my sister was barely born, when my father drove me to her house in the night so that my mother did not have to hear us both crying. I cried because I wanted to help, but did not yet have enough words to say so.

I asked her, later, where her songs came from, but she didn't tell me. She just passed me another jar of summer squash to put onto the top shelf, where she couldn't reach any more, and said that I should look in the place where fall began and summer ended, if indeed they were the same place, and that maybe I would find her songs there.

My grandmother lined the shelves of her cold cellar with old song sheets from the Christmas newspaper. In between the printed lyrics, she sometimes pencilled lines of different songs. But the sheets were cut apart, so as to fit on the shelves, and I could never find their beginnings.

❧

I should have learned about canning from my grandmother. I helped her with the pickles when I was younger, going to farmers' markets on rainy days.

We went there together as soon as I got to her house. I was in my reversible raincoat and shorter than everyone, hurrying from stall to stall, standing in the damp while my grandmother traded paper dollar bills for tomatoes and little cucumbers in brown bags and bushel baskets. The tarps over the stalls turned the rain into a tap, gushing at the edges and turned off but still dripping underneath. It was outdoors, in the morning, but I remember everything as dark, with concrete underfoot.

When I dream about it, sometimes the pickles are in green baskets and sometimes they are in brown ones. The green ones are plastic and look like they're made from giant pickles with holes where the bumps should be.

We went home, half an hour by car away, though I don't remember us driving. She put the giant pot on the stove, black with light speckles, a robin's egg in negative. There were jars with rubber rings and glass lids; silver screw tops sat on the window ledge after we washed them in a bucket of lemony soap and rinsed them by holding them out the door into the rain.

The cucumbers had bumps that felt spiky to my fingertips and soft to the backs of my hands. I sat outside in the rain and scrubbed them under the leak in the eavestrough and then put them in the crock. I liked being trusted. When I was cooking vegetables with my mother, she washed them again when she thought I wasn't looking.

We floated the pink plate on top of the pickles, and weighed it down with a jar of last year's pickles to keep everything from popping up and not getting enough taste inside them. Then my grandmother read me the jokes from the back of her magazines and I made necklaces from buttons.

I was too young, then, to remember how to make the pickles now. And my grandmother is too old, now, to remember how she made the pickles then. So my grandfather says that he helps her, and that my cousins help, too. But they scrub the pickles and he chops them and measures out the seasoning and moves them from the crock to the jars and plunges the jars into the boiling water with his hands, which never get burned. My grandmother only measures the green colouring into the pickles, while my grandfather watches and adds more after she leaves to rest her eyes.

❧

Here,
in the place where I push air in
and you push it back out,
where it is not sure
whether it is coming
or going
(and, perhaps, neither are we),
is the same place that we met
once
to learn about—

But you've forgotten that day—
you should, if you haven't already

❧

Yeast is made from sadness, my grandmother told me.

I went home after she told me this and asked my mother if it was true. She said of course it wasn't, that yeast is made of fungus (and here she showed me a picture from her textbook, of yeast and yeast's relatives, who I pictured as tiny fungus families living inside bread-houses, inspiring a vow that I kept for seven hours to never eat bread again). You cannot make things from sadness, my mother continued, except for artwork. All art is made from sadness—just look at your father.

I was unclear as to whether my father was supposed to be a work of art, and he was made from sadness, or if it was my father's artwork that was made from sadness. If it were the latter, I didn't know where he got the sadness from, as he made very many pieces of art and hardly ever seemed to be sad, except when my mother put up her hair to go to work and made it seem straight instead of curly.

I went to my grandmother's house again the day after she told me about yeast, and I told her that my mother said yeast is not made from sadness, it is made of fungus. I had even traced the picture of yeast and its relatives from my mother's textbook into my school notebook and taken it from home to school to my grandmother's house in order to show her. This is irrefutable evidence, I told my grandmother. Yeast is made of fungus. (Every day when my father came down from his studio in the attic, he brought with him a new word, in the same way that other fathers bring home presents from their business trips or chocolate from the office vending machine. Three days ago my father had brought home *irrefutable*, and this was my first chance to try it out.)

We are going to make bread, said my

grandmother. I promise to teach you nothing about fungus, but when we are finished, you will know how to bake with sadness. I said that I had no sadness and neither did my father, and I thought perhaps that was why neither one of us made bread.

What about your mother? said my grandmother. I said that my mother made bread sometimes, but always at work. She grew the yeast in her lab and baked the bread while she was waiting for her experiments to finish. Until my confusion the day before, I had never wondered what she grew the yeast out of; yesterday, I spent half the day picturing Petri dishes full of sad movies and the other half imagining the drawing from the textbook somehow sprung to life inside a forest of test tubes growing on a rack in the lab's kitchen.

My grandmother asked which bread tasted better, the bread that my mother brought home from her laboratory or the bread that I had at my grandmother's after school. I told her that hers tasted better, not because she was there and my mother wasn't, but because it was true. I later developed this thought into a theory that some things can only be made properly once one becomes a grandmother—bread, gravy, and turkey stuffing chief among them. When I told my grandmother of my theory, she said that it had nothing to do with being a grandmother and everything to do with accumulating enough sadness to put in your bread and still have some left to cry over.

While we talked about my mother, my grandmother got out the ingredients for bread and lined them up on the counter: flour, sugar, yeast, salt, lard, milk.

I ripped open the tiny packet of yeast along the edge of its yellow stripe, and poured it into the small bowl that my grandmother held out. She cupped her hand and poured sugar into it from the Redpath bag, and tossed it on top of the yeast. She filled the bowl halfway with water, and said *enough* when I asked how much water and sugar to put in. The yeast eats the sugar, she said, that's how it grows. Sadness eats the sweet memories that make it seem sadder in comparison, she said, that's how it grows.

My grandmother scooped the lard from its bucket and dropped it in a pot, and poured the milk on top. She sprinkled in some sugar and some salt. She heated them on the stove.

We heat until the fat is just melted, said my grandmother. I asked her why there was no recipe for her bread. My mother used a recipe—I knew this because once when I was too sick to go to school, she took me to her laboratory with her. I don't know why I didn't just stay with my father in his studio, which is what I usually did, perhaps he was away showing pictures at an exhibition. At any rate, he was gone and my grandmother must have been gone, too, because I went with my mother and it was Friday, which was the day for bread.

My mother had various page holders which stood by the machines that analyzed her experiments. Mostly they held notes for experiments or pages headed *Call for Papers! Results of Study In!*, but one had on it a recipe for bread. It sat behind the other paper holders, underneath the painting of my father's on the wall next to the door, and looked like it did not belong, which, perhaps, it did not. I was small enough to sleep on two of the lab's chairs pushed fronts together, and my mother brought in blankets and pillows and pieces of stale bread from last week to nibble on, and I lay in the lab beside the fume hood, watching her make bread and experiments as I dozed away my sickness. She always checked with the recipe, which she said came from my aunt, my grandmother's sister. I never asked why she did not use my grandmother's non-recipe instead.

Do you have a recipe for sadness? said my grandmother. Then why do you expect me to have a recipe for something made of sadness and flour?

We poured the milk into a bowl and I stirred it to make it cool faster. The yeast kept getting larger, bubbling almost out of its bowl.

That is the reason that when you are sad, the sadness bubbles up inside of you, because sadness is yeasty, said my grandmother. And if there is nowhere for it to go, it will sit inside your belly and expand inside your stomach until there is no other thing for it but to grow into the corridor of your throat, where it will sit until it escapes as a sob or until it is temporarily delayed by a glass of cold water.

We poured the yeast into the milk, once it had cooled, and stirred. My grandmother added flour, a cup at a time, while I stirred until my arms were not strong enough any more and then I added flour, a quarter cup at a time, while she stirred, her hands that were both mixers and pistons plunged into the dough.

I asked my grandmother why she had never told my mother that yeast was made of sadness. She said that she did not know until much after my mother would have believed her, and that she and I were closer in age than she and my mother were. I told her I did not understand, and she told me that I did not understand bread, either, and that one day I would forget that yeast was made of sadness and forget how to make bread and start believing in the irrefutable evidence for fungus-yeast, and that then I would know why she had never told my mother. I told her that I believed her, and that her evidence was more irrefutable than my mother's. I said that I would not forget. She handed me the empty bowl and told me to wash it while she floured the counter.

My grandmother kneaded the bread and tore off a corner for me to knead, too. We kneaded, she on the floor with a butcher block under her feet to lift her up, and I on the chair brought in from the dining room.

I asked her why, if yeast was made from sadness, did tears taste like salt and not like yeast? She laughed and said that I would understand once I understood how to make bread.

We punched down the bread and let it rise, then punched it down again and let it rise again, sitting on top of the radiator so that it would be warm despite the coldness of the kitchen. We baked six loaves, each the same size, except for one that was smaller and looked like I had made it.

I took home one loaf of bread, and at dinner that night, we ate my loaf and my mother's loaf. We could tell which one was hers because she always put crosses in the top. My father brought down a new picture and hung it over the kitchen table, on the wall on top of the window. He said it was called sadness, and it was a picture of me and a loaf of bread. I told him that I did not understand.

Years later, I told my own granddaughter why tears taste like salt instead of yeast. I thought that the age when you can understand bread is far too late to understand sadness. Tears taste like salt because salt is the ingredient that stops yeast from rising forever.

❧

Can I look at your insides, I asked her, between pickles and learning about sadness and other things that I have forgotten, thinking that she would say I wasn't old enough yet or that we could do it later, which meant never.

She said yes, instead. I asked her again because I didn't believe her, though I wanted to, and she said nothing, only rolled up the sleeve of the flowered blouse that she wore on Saturdays when she knew that she was going out in the evening and wouldn't have time to change between finishing the bread and my grandfather getting home with his suit on, ready for their dancing lessons. My grandfather wouldn't be home for another hour, at least.

She unbuttoned the skin below the crook of her elbow while she warmed the soup on the stove. The inside of her skin was bumpy but wanted to be smooth, like the pages of a book dropped into water and then dried again. To see if the soup is hot enough, you should taste it, she said. Your fingers cannot tell the difference between warm and ready.

She lifted up her skin, tugging at the edges where the seams were. It separated in a line, like perforated coupon edges, except for a little section near her wrist that broke off into crumbs on the countertop.

The bones of the soup stock stuck out above the liquid and the broth bubbled over them, popping little droplets onto the white enamel of the stove. She rolled her skin down to her wrist and snapped a rubber band tight over it to stop it from rolling up again.

She unbuttoned her other arm the same, pulled at the edges, rolled it into a scroll at her wrist held down by an elastic. The insides of her arms were brown, like the dark rye bread at the bakery in town where we would go when company was coming for dinner.

She told me to add some pepper to the soup.

She rubbed her hands together, loosening her skin's hold on her body, she said. She tugged at her fingertips and slid them up over her fingernails, covering them with skin so that her nail polish only showed through when she held her hands up to the light. The piece between her wrist and her hand pulled up was coloured somewhere between rye bread and raw meat, the brown colour of the chopping block when you've waited too long to clean up after dinner.

She apologized that it looked like the flesh of an old woman. She said that my insides were much lighter, unripened. If you looked inside your mother, she said, she would be perfectly ripe. Your sister's insides are the palest of all, because they have not yet begun to ripen. Yours are pink, the same colour as the walls of your room.

She unrolled the skin at her wrists, moistened it with the steam from the soup, and pressed it back down onto her arms, wetting the edges so that the seam was barely visible. She pulled her hands back together, then picked the bones out of the soup and left them outside the door for the neighbours' dog.

That night, I dreamed that we ate roast beef sandwiches on rye bread, on a night when my grandmother was gone.

❧

Some days later, she had all the ingredients out for bread.

But I thought you were making pickles this week, I said.

She said we were making a person instead, out of flour and yeast and the cracked grains that she bought at the store with the green sign and the wooden floors that creaked near the doors and the shelves. She said that the pickles were started and that there was nothing to do for them until after tomorrow.

She said we would add dirt from the garden to make her real. Women are made from bread and dirt, she said, and yeast from the kitchen and water from the rain make them grow. That is why we all have sadness inside us, she said, because we cannot grow without yeast.

We will make her from dough, and plant her in the garden, she said. I asked her if my mother was lying, if my sister was made from bread and earth and not from parts of my father stuck inside my mother's belly. I asked her how I was made, too, if I was made from parts or from bread.

Your mother did not lie, said my grandmother. But we are making a woman. She will not be a child, like you, and will never be small enough to have a mother.

There is a space between you and me, she said, that you will leap over in your sleep, when you are on the edge of waking someday. You will not know when you have left your young self behind, and you will not know when you have first met your old self. You will not know when the dirt that is on your hands from the garden starts being part of your skin, and you will not know when the bread you have eaten starts to bubble inside you.

But the woman we are making will not have a young self. Earth will always be part of her skin, and sadness will always be inside her belly. Her childhood will be yeast and water, fermenting inside the earth. When will she be born, I asked. How will she get out of the ground, with no one underground to push her? Will she be a woman like you, or like my mother?

She will be a daughter of the earth, said my grandmother, she will be born when we both are earth, and we will feed her as she grows. But she will not be born from talking.

And my grandmother ripped the yellow packet of yeast, and emptied it into a bowl with some sugar, and filled it with enough warm water from the tap. She sent me into the garden to gather dirt from beside the tulips.

She will climb out of the ground on the roots of the trees, said my grandmother.

We mixed the earth in with the flour, in the big ceramic bowl that my grandfather brought her from the island. We added the cracked grain from the canvas sack at the bottom of the cupboard, too.

And when she is grown, the only difference between her and you is that she will not remember why she is sad, said my grandmother. You should never forget your sadness, she said, because then you will have forgotten your childhood.

We melted the butter, mixed it with molasses, and added more water. We added the yeast and sugar. We stirred. My grandmother sent me out for more dirt from the yard.

But when will she be born, I asked? How will we know that she is born, if we are not here to see her?

We won't. And my grandmother kept stirring, while I poured in flour and dirt and grain. We let her rise while we went out to pick tulips for my aunt.

We punched down the dough, and it left smudges on our hands. Instead of getting out the loaf pans, my grandmother got out a burlap sheet, and we made her in pieces.

Her head was a round ball, thinner on the top than on the bottom, larger than my fist and smaller than my head. We braided the tops of her arms, and twisted the bottom halves. They are braided and twisted for strength, said my grandmother.

We made her belly with a hole in the middle and a pouch at the bottom. We hadn't mixed the earth in all the way, and her belly was dirtier than all the rest.

We made her legs from one piece, cut down the middle. Her hands and feet were bulges at the end of her arms and legs, her back was only the reverse of her belly. Her eyes were holes with grain in the centre.

She had a second rising, sitting on the burlap, in the window under the light. Then we dug a hole in the backyard, next to a tree with big roots, so that she could climb out. She would climb out and go home, said my grandmother, and she would know she was there when someone asked her why she was sad and loved her anyway when she couldn't answer.

I was never entirely sure if she was real, if we had made a woman who would be born from the aging of yeast in the belly of the earth, after we both were dead. And by the time I was old enough to know that she was not real, that people are made only from parts of boys stuck inside women's stomachs and not from dirt and sadness, it had happened too long ago for me to be certain that it wasn't a dream. When I asked my grandmother about it, she didn't remember. She had forgotten it, or at least had pretended to forget, in order not to embarrass my grandfather.

❧

Some time after she taught me how to make bread, my grandmother started to die. I knew that she was dying because she called me the name of her dead sister, my great-aunt Marguerite, when I was leaving her house. She had told me once that when you begin to die, you must forget everyone you are leaving behind. That you must be very careful to erase their names from your lips and the feel of their faces from your hands and the sound of their voices from your ears and the smell of their shoulders from your nose. She said that if you did not, if you remembered them when you were dead, that you would want to come back to them and could not really die until you had forgotten them. It was much easier to forget while you were still alive, she said, because you could replace the living with those already dead. Once you were dead there were no aids to forgetting.

I was worried, at first, that my mother would start dying, too. She went to my grandmother's house between her laboratory and our house, even though it was not on the way. She would drive there in her silver car and say mmm-hmm when I asked her why she did not bike to my grandmother's like she used to when she would visit my grandmother by herself every Saturday. (I wondered, then, if she was driving so that she could take my grandmother's body with her if she died while my mother was at her house. I never imagined where she would take it, but it certainly would not fit in the basket on her bike or in the satchel that she would bring home, full of sweets, each time she visited my grandmother on her own.)

Once, when I was still worried that both my mother and my grandmother had started dying, and almost believed dying to be contagious, I went to my grandmother's house. I asked her why she did not have to forget everything when she died, only people. She said that she would forget everything, one day, but that it was not time to forget those things yet. She still needed to remember food so that she could feed my grandfather, who had not yet begun dying. She still needed to remember people, even, so that we would not all think that she was dead already.

She wished she could remember the newest people, she said, because most of them were still alive. But the oldest people were the hardest to unremember, because their inertia of memory was greatest. My grandmother did not say inertia of memory. I remembered it that way afterwards, because I was just starting to learn about physics.

She stopped using recipes, once she knew she was dying. She said that she needed to forget how to read, because the knowing took up too much space. The only things she remembered were the things that she had never written down. Bread, and stuffing, and the buns with little pools of jam in the middle.

My grandfather knew how to cook, suddenly. He made the pickles and put them in the jars so that my grandmother could rest her eyes, he said. But she didn't seem to be resting, I thought. She looked like she was dying, which is much harder work.

When you are dying (I know this because my grandmother told me, much before she started to die), you must always be thinking. You must always shut the doors on memories that threaten to open and catch your foot as you are running towards death. Those open doors will slow you down, my grandmother said, and you can't have that. Dying is already slow enough without courting days and summer picnics and fairs in the autumn holding at your ankles and reminding you why, until now, you've been running away from death instead of towards it.

When my great-aunt Marguerite, who I never met, was dying from the hole in her heart, my mother and my grandmother went to visit her in the hospital. She had wires and boxes on top of her and underneath her before they got there, but my grandmother told the nurses to take them all away. She told me that you need space to throw off the last of your memories, since they are the ones that stick the most. But if your arms are surrounded by tubes and your mouth is covered in a mask, then you can't throw them away or even blow them out when they come up your throat and remind you by their taste of the things you must leave behind. So when my mother came in, my great-aunt Marguerite was alone, with flowers beside her and my grandmother holding her hand.

She sort of shrunk, like an old balloon, said my mother, when she was recounting the story. Your grandmother, my momma, rolled up Aunt Marguerite's fingers inside her hand and squeezed, like the end of an almost-used-up tube of toothpaste. And while your grandmother squeezed, they breathed out, together. But only your grandmother breathed in again.

We went home afterwards, and no one else was there, said my mother. We had pickles out of the pink dish, and chocolate ice cream, after. I wasn't allowed to tell anyone what we ate, since it was winter, and ice cream is summer food. You're the only one who knows, my mother said.

You must always finish by breathing out, said my grandmother, when she was recounting the story. If you breathe in at the last, then you will take whatever is there in the room with you. Marguerite almost did not breathe out, at the end, except I squeezed her hand to remind her. That is why, when you go to sleep, you count your breaths, and always breathe out on the last one. So that if you die, you do not take your bedroom with you and have to come back to leave it behind.

We went back to the house and had pickles, said my grandmother. We ate the last jar, from the small pink dish, and I washed it right away so that your grandfather wouldn't know. He always wanted to have a jar left, in case there weren't any cucumbers next year.

Your…aunt Marguerite said that she was going home when she died, said my grandmother. I laughed at her, she continued, pretended that home could not be anywhere but here, where we were already, with the wires and metal boxes gone, in this hospital in the city. I said that she was already home, that I was there, and your mother was there, and that what more did you need for home than people who you belonged to?

But she knew something, then, said my grandmother, that I did not know until I, too, started to die: that you spend your whole life where you belong, but often you don't belong to home.

And then she died. And we went back to our house, and we ate the pickles in the pink dish and said that we would be at home when people called to see where they could bring flowers and hot plates in crockery dishes and old birthday cards that they meant to send but had forgotten. We sat there, your mother and I, amongst the detritus of mourning, but we were not at home.

And then I knew where home was, and more than anything I wanted to go home, she said. But I couldn't then, because your mother needed looking after and your grandfather was coming back from the farm soon. And you can't go now, and I am almost ready to, but not yet, and your mother might have gone home, once, but she never did and now she will have to wait until she is dying. And you belong here, she said, as we belonged there, in the spaces between the kindness of casseroles, and your mother belongs where she is, in her lab and your father's arms; we all belong here, but it will never be home for any of us.

There are a few who are lucky. Their homes are where they belong. And another few who belong near enough to home that they can visit every once in awhile, and some who belong somewhere where they can, once, scrape together enough time and money to visit home, even if they can't stay. And some who belong far enough away from home that they don't even know that they're missing anything.

And then there's you and me, she said, the luckiest and the worst. We belong far enough away that we can never visit, but close enough that we can just see it on the horizon. So we will never forget that we are not home, but we will never go home, either.

You thought when you were younger that your home was at my house, she said.

I told her that we were home, here, that she always called it home in the stories she told, and that she hadn't been lying in the stories so she must be mistaken now. We were at home, and there was bread in the oven and pickles in the crock in the basement, and my grandfather was getting home soon, so we should get dinner on.

That was the last time we cooked together.

Some days, later, I would put the already-baked bread in the oven to warm; I would clear the table and wash the dishes with the silver edges that meant the day was important.

But my grandfather, who always had a habit of interrupting, would pour the milk onto the scalloped potatoes and check to see if the turkey was done and suddenly there was only room in the kitchen for my grandfather to stand and my grandmother to sit on the stool with the kick-down footrest.

I started making preserves on my own, after I went away to school, in the time after my grandmother started dying.

The instructions were from my mother's best friend. Her mother came to stay with her in the summers and they canned together while her husband and her father fixed the broken boards in their backyard fence.

She gave me the tomatoes, too, a bushel basket in a cardboard box. I thought that it wouldn't take long, and I started just after I should have fallen asleep, thinking that I would finish before morning and still sleep enough to dream.

But memories get compressed, foreshortened. They must get smaller, shave time from their recall, turn tricks of light and shadow to make space enough for all of them to fit; a task that took a day now seems an hour's work.

I canned all night.

I dreamed before I slept, instead. I saw pictures in the steam from the blanching tomatoes and imagined that the sun was rising in the oven as I watched the orange element sterilize the jars. I cut up peppers and pears, peaches and onions, and my onion tears diluted the tomato juice pooling on the stove. I chopped vegetables and cut cheesecloth for the spices past midnight.

I added the vegetables and the fruit, savoury and sweet, with the vinegar and sugar, sour and sweet, to the pot. I left the lid on while it boiled, and fell asleep on the floor against the refrigerator. I didn't know that the chutney couldn't thicken unless the pot was open and the tomato-water could steam off.

I took the lid off and fell asleep on the floor again, folded up between the front of the fridge and the door of the oven, my back cold and the soles of my feet too hot, the egg timer balanced between my legs and my belly.

When it was finished, I poured the chutney through a funnel into the jars that I bought at the supermarket. My mother's best friend gave me the funnel, too; it belonged to her grandmother.

I lay on the couch as the sun was rising, listening to the popping as the jars sealed on the counter. I forgot to turn off the oven, with the tall jar that I didn't need still left inside. It cracked along the bottom after I fell asleep.

&

She will not die for another seven years, at least that's what it said when I read about it in a book. Dying is different than death, I think, because death just happens, and then it's over, and there's no time to prepare—even if you have prepared, whatever you've done is not enough. Death is something that anyone can do; dying is only for those who know how to pack for it.

Dying is like preparing for a trip, but you never know when the train is going to leave. Every night you lay out your travelling clothes and put your glasses on the table beside your bed so that you can find them if it's dark out when you leave. You check the list of emergency telephone numbers and walk to the neighbours' to leave them a key so that they can water the plants. You consult the train schedule and write down the number of your track. And when you wake up and it's not the day to leave yet, you cross off that day's track number and replace it with tomorrow's, and you check the day after that, just to make sure the train will still be running if you're delayed again. But you never know. You only know that if you haven't crossed off every item on the list, that if you leave your glasses on the desk instead of beside your bed, that the trip will happen, and you'll have to go, but you won't have your travelling clothes on.

So you dress every morning in the same travelling clothes and you never do anything that will take longer than a day, because you wouldn't want the pickles to be left half-finished, without the jars sealed, if you have to go away.

three

How do you describe a time when words are lost?

How do you outline the shape of flesh already disappearing within skin, create a new skin and a new flesh from newspaper and breadcrusts, stuff words into dry mouths and press memories into hands that want only comfort?

I cannot tell you, for the words to tell with are gone. I cannot even make a rubbing of their traces, for I fear that their memory will fade with the gentle pressure of my chalk.

%

The last thing she forgot was how to speak. Not her earliest memory, perhaps, but one of the most enduring.

She still hummed, still turned her head when I spoke, still suckled the proffered spoon of squash soup warmed over from last fall's final batch—but none of these are memories, skills, things stored away. They are only the beginnings of things (or the endings of things), the urges that expand into learning and contract again into forgetfulness.

Tired of travelling on the increasingly slow conveyor between mind and mouth, the last of her words had fallen from her lips and dribbled down into the folds of her sweater, crumbs to be shaken out before the next wearing. They joined the first abandoned words, the ones that hid themselves in the pages of newspapers or in messages on ditto pads, waiting to be discovered once or twice again before they left for good. They joined the names with vowels switched, the words repeated, but with different meaning each time. They left behind a skeletal syntax, the beginnings of a grammar that were also the end, the scaffolding surrounding nothing, perfectly constructed.

She had already stopped reading, of course. At first she read the newspaper every day, pouring words into her sieve almost faster than they could empty out the bottom. She read even the sections she hated, the sports and the business, reading and keeping the words in her head and making new memories to replace the ones that she lost.

She underlined headlines and clipped out the ones that she thought we should see, pressed them into our palms, our pockets, the handbags we left on the chair in the hall while we sat in the kitchen with tea. She mailed them with letters, with writing across the top, above the headlines, telling us to use this and see this and remember this when you are doing the wash or the cooking or going to school tomorrow. I am making a scrapbook, she would say, of things I would like you to remember.

And so she started her scrapbook, cutting out articles and pasting them in, at first only ones she had read, but then later the ones that she didn't have time for. For later, she would say, I'll read them later, when I have time. But now I must bake the bread for your grandfather and heat up the soup from yesterday for dinner and put the meat on. I haven't the time for reading, she would say.

I believed her, at first.

She began to cut out the words, making sentences like six-year-olds, with gaps where their teeth should have been. I am coming to see you, she said, coming on the—

And so I would go to the bus station and my mother to the train station, and then I would see her and I would say hello, I am so glad you came, and why don't we go to the train station and watch the trains come in, won't that be wonderful?

And so we would go, and there was my mother, her daughter, what a pleasant surprise, I would say, we should go for tea.

Yes, tea, she would say. That would be—

She did not ask us to remember for her, to remind her when she forgot, because she did not forget, she only made copies of her memory from paper and photographs, kneaded it into the bread she was baking and stirred it into the soup on the stove full of whispers.

This is a word I do not recognize, she would say, can you teach me what it means? And so I taught her, and she grabbed it back for a moment, grabbed the slippery word that was harder to catch than the light, and repeated the word again so she could hold it. But each time it repeated it was slippery, sliding, harder to catch.

She threw it back, then, asked me to show her again, what does this word mean to say?

We played catch with the light and the words, in the evening, at the end of the day.

༄

This is my favourite time, the time when the year is dying. The days are getting shorter and shorter, and we light the candles earlier, and still earlier—to welcome or ward off the darkness, I am not sure which.

I did not notice it getting darker today until I looked up from the book I was reading—I thought I heard you at the window—and looked back, and could see only grey stripes where the words used to be.

It was silly to look up—I couldn't have heard you at the window. You are here, beside me, tearing yesterday's paper into thinner and thinner strips, reading—or imagining you are reading—the words down each strip:

turn the taxi/to the lounge/to boogie-woogie./

13 more times/his albums sold/numbers with/Benny/Ella/Lester/DeFranco./

was the trio/famous threesome/work written/later wrote./

four times and had/his first and third/with his fourth./

continued/because, as he/I think I/over the years./

having/more playing/he told/sit down/I want it to./

I should turn the lamp on for you.

You were not at the window. If I heard anyone, it was the boy who comes to deliver flyers, though he usually comes before dark. Or it was the robin you fed too late, tricked into thinking he has found his home for the winter. Or it was nothing, the wind in the trees we have yet to trim, their branches banging to be let in.

Today was sunny twice: once from the sky, and again reflected from the snow. The days are short but brilliant, and we get up early in the dark so that we do not miss any part of the day. What will you have on your toast for breakfast, I ask, eggs, or jam and peanut butter?

Toast, toast; I will make the toast, you say, and pull out the drawer with the bread in it.

You remind me of the man who came up from Quebec when my mother was small, who boarded with you on the farm and worked from dark 'til dark again. He couldn't speak a lick of English, you would say, when telling a story about him. Well, that's not entirely true dear, says my grandfather, he knew a few words. And none of them fit for company!, you reply.

But he was a good worker, a good man, you repeat, he didn't know a lick of English though. The children would try to teach him, they would point and say the words—bread, knife, butter, plate, jam—each time waiting for him to say them back. Bread, breed. Knife, neuf. Butter, butteh. Plate, pleut. Jam, gem. Oh, it was funny to hear him talk!—to hear him taste the words, rolling them up inside his tongue like tobacco in his cigarette papers, sealing them against falling out, against forgetting.

And they would laugh—oh, how they would laugh!—when he heard a word that they had taught him and tried to understand. He grabbed the words he knew from their conversations, repeating and repeating and repeating, trying to find a whole sentence within a single word, smiling when they laughed.

Toast, toast, you say, I will make the toast.

You are angry to discover that I have thrown away the stale crusts you put in a bag at the back of the drawer. What if I need those? you ask, what if I need those for something?

And then you forget—first what you needed them for and then what it was that you needed.

Eggs it is! I say, and start the eggs. I start the toast, too, since you have gone to sit in the chair by the fire, nodding off beside the flames just awakened for the day.

It is my favourite time of year, I tell you, though I doubt you are listening. It is the time when the year is dying. The nights are getting colder and colder, and spring is too far ahead to see and too long past to remember.

It seems as if it will never be warm again, you say—smiling at something I cannot see. It seems as if it will always get colder and colder. But I will tell you a secret! By the time the coldest days arrive, the year is already being born again—the chills are shudders of awakening, an engine turning over in the dark.

We get up early and eat our breakfast in the kitchen, watching the streetlamp patterns on the wall disappear as the sun rises. You pile scrambled eggs onto your toast, simultaneously fastidious and unaware you have dropped half of them onto the floor. I pour your tea.

After breakfast, we stand at the sink and wash dishes. You fill an extra bin with water and set it on the counter for rinsing, and soak the eggy pan at the bottom of the sink while you wash the plates and forks. I take the dishes when you are done, dunk them in the bucket, wrap them and dry them in soft towels that are older than I am, and stack them in the cupboard that I still do not believe I can reach into, though its door is now level with my eyes.

We finish and walk back to the living room, and you pause by the oven to open its door. You breathe in, confused, and then keep walking.

You sit again in your chair by the fire, and pick up the newspaper that I left on the stool for you. I do not think you will notice that it is a few days old, and you do not; you pick it up and say let's see what is happening today, my dear, which part would you like?

The grey light that fills both morning and late afternoon this time of year is pressed back into the windows by the fire. I take the section that you offer me, but do not read it; I pick up the book that I started yesterday instead. You glance at me once in a while, and we smile, and you get up to stoke the fire, or to put more wood in through the door at the side.

The day turns brighter and then darker again, and the letters of my book blur in the grey light. You are talking to yourself now, smiling and nodding along to your words.

I just like to sit with my feet up, you say, with my feet up beside the fire. I like to build a little fire; your grandfather keeps the wood outside the door so that I can build myself a little fire. It's nice to have your feet up beside the fire. And at this, you point at your knees and say, my feet don't bend as well as they used to, that's why your grandfather keeps the wood right outside the door, so I don't have to crouch down behind the woodshed to get the wood for the fire. It's so nice to put your feet up beside the fire.

ஃ

Some years before the toast and the dishes and the newspaper torn into strips, I was helping my father with painting. He loved to paint without thinking, he said, and so in the summers, when his attic studio became too hot, he walked down the street of our house, knocking on the doors of our neighbours, and offering to paint their homes.

He painted for free, told them they only needed to buy the paint and he would paint for them. They tried to pay him, with cash slipped into his canvas apron when he took it off to eat lunch, with cookies and casseroles on our doorstep when he slipped the cash back through the mail slot, folded into little paper frogs and cranes. He paid me for helping him, but never with their money, always with his own.

I was helping my father with painting, at the house of my grandfather's friend—a man my grandfather had known since before he and my grandmother were married. We were painting the house the colour of nakedness; the paint that dried on our clothes looked like slashes in the fabric, revealing opaque, artificial skin.

I was high up on the ladder, underneath an awning, with the bucket hanging from a bent clothes hanger beneath me, swinging slightly each time I dipped my paintbrush. I painted the edges of the wall next to the roof, sealing against leaks and abrasions. My father stood beneath me, his giant brush covering great swaths of the house in skin that glistened, for a moment, like ours, sweating in the heat of the day.

I fell off the ladder. My father had gone to

say that we were breaking for lunch, and the ladder slipped down the wall, and I slipped down the ladder; the bucket of paint fell on top of me, covering me in drops of skin.

My father still had houses to paint and exhibitions to attend, and my mother was in her laboratory, and so I went to my grandmother's house. It seemed farther away, then, than it does now, and I lay stretched across the back seat for the journey, a bandage the colour that my skin used to be wrapped around my swollen, purple ankle.

I stayed there for a week, with my ankle getting brighter and smaller, the purple skin receding into purple, green, yellow, brown spots, my grandmother rubbing salve on my ankle before bed and plunging my foot into buckets of ice, then hot water, holding it beneath the surface while I opened and closed my fists. She told me stories of my mother's childhood injuries, which were worse than my own, because her grandmother was dead by the time she could walk, and my grandmother was not yet a grandmother, and thus not yet able to draw healing from the air, only from the powders and salves that had to last the childhood of many children.

I would like this to be my last memory of my grandmother. But it is not.

(I do not have a last memory of her, only a collage of days increasingly the same and the sense, in silent moments, that I have forgotten something.)

❧

This is the last time you will have this memory.

If only there was a warning, a lamp that was lit, a pressure in the space between your belly and your lungs, a taste on your tongue when you inhaled, telling you, reminding you that when you exhale, when you fall asleep, when you turn the corner, that you will no longer have this memory.

Something to give you time, pencil and paper and a surface to write on, time to write it down, time to tell your husband, your daughter, your granddaughter, time to save your memory although you cannot keep it.

Or perhaps there could be no warning, and no ghost of memory either. If only it could slip away, unnoticed, if only you could forget that it was forgotten.

But you forget, and only remember enough to know that you have forgotten. You are haunted but not comforted, troubled with no possibility of calm. Your only certainty is that there was a word, once, or a phrase, a word to describe the picture in the hallway, a word for the jars with the old cucumbers inside.

I thought for a while that you did not remember. That you did not know, any more, what you used to be like. But I know now that all you remember is forgetting, that you cry in the night when you think everyone else is asleep, that you only remember that you must hide your shame, and you feel only shame because you cannot hide it.

We will make new memories, I said, a new memory for today, and tomorrow, and the next day. We will make new memories together, you and I. And so I get out the recipe that you have written for me, the recipe that you never needed, that you made only because I was not wise enough, yet, to know by the taste at the beginning how things will turn out in the end, to know that this bitterness now will be mellow and sweet a little later. So I get out the recipe, and ask you for the flour, and you point me to the garden.

We will make new memories, you and I, we will go out and pick the flowers that you planted before I was born, that remember to come back every year, even after their names are forgotten. We will pick the flowers to set on the table, to make it beautiful. And then I will get out the recipe again, and ask you for the flour, and you will point me to the cupboard. Pour this, I will say, and I will rip the packet of yeast and hand it to you, and you will pour it into the bowl with the warm water and the sugar, stir it around, and say that it smells like home again. You will smile at me, and lean over the bowl to smell the yeast growing, to smell the smell of home again. Home again, you will say again. Home again. I will heat the milk on the stove, you will tell me to be careful, be careful, because that is what you say when someone uses the stove, be careful. The stove and the oven, and the pit for the fire in the yard, be careful, you'll say, be careful.

We scald the milk and pour it into the bowl from the island, pour it along the sides, and you stir it to make it cool, and we add the yeast, and the flour to make a sponge. And you lean over the bowl again and smile at me, and say this smells like home again. And we add the egg and the fat and the salt, and you stir while I pour; now I am taller and you are short. I pour while you stir, and then I stir when you cannot stir any more. And then we take out the dough, and I rip off a corner for you.

It will rise, you say, it will rise with the heat of the morning (though it is spring and the mornings are still cool). It will rise in the window, you say, not because you remember why, but because this bowl belongs in the window, because you do not remember, but you know that something is out of place. And so we put it in the window, and I do not bother to tell you that you used to make bread in the afternoon, and this window faces west.

Tomorrow we will make a new memory, I tell you, a new memory for you and for me.

We will make soup tomorrow, I tell you, soup with the last of this winter's squash, and we will can it to save it until the squash comes again. But you cannot hold the knife, anymore, to cut the squash, and you cannot peel the potatoes or the parsnips, and so you sit, on your stool, waiting for me to peel the carrots and cut them so that you can drop them, one by one, into the broth with the leeks and the onions. You stand at the sink and wash the leeks, peeling back the green ribbons and holding them up to the tap, scrubbing them with the pads of your fingers, cleaning half of them and missing the other half. You stand at the sink while I chop the onions, cleaning the leeks and setting them, carefully, on the butcher's block.

I think you are crying, but perhaps it is only the onions.

We leave the soup to simmer, and sit outside where it is still too cold to sit, and you tuck another blanket around my legs, though I have already brought one from inside.

It has been a long time since I had little ones, you say. It has been a long time since I had young ones of my own.

We are sitting on the porch, outside, where it is too cold to sit, and I am worrying that the frost will come—only once more, or twice, but once would be enough—and that your flowers will die until next year.

✤

And so we sit here, you and I.

Until I forget and you remember.

Until the poles reverse

and summer is winter

and the leaves grow back into the trees.

We will sit here while the world unmakes itself

and the sheets are pulled tight and tucked underneath the bed.

We will sit here and wait for you to remember the word

for your forgetting.

I forget why we are sitting here, grandmother.

I forget why you left for the kitchen and came back with your hands empty.

I forget which key belongs to the lock on the front door, and which to the lock on the cabinet.

You have forgotten we are sitting here at all.

☙

There is a small, white, withered part of her finger, the part underneath the ring. It is wrinkly to look at and smooth and soft to touch, like the skin of a nectarine. The rest of her hands are wrinkled to see and wrinkled to touch, flabby and drooping down, doll's hands without enough stuffing.

I do not remember what I was going to say about the ring, whether it was to be a symbol of something covering, something hiding, or whether the flesh beneath it was to be a metaphor for something lost and found again, just in time at the end. Or whether I was noting it as the only smooth place left in a body of crags and wrinkles.

We took off the ring and put it on a chain around her neck to stop her from pulling it off and pushing it on. Pulling and pushing and scraping against the skin of her knuckles, the wrinkly and never smooth parts. Pulling and pushing and rubbing the rest of her finger smooth and then wet and then bleeding.

She had always kept her hands busy, busy with bread and busy with soup, busy with fixing and healing and making lives out of nothing but bits of earth and yeast.

Busyness is not the right word, exactly, busy and doing are different things. Her hands were always doing things, necessary things. Busyness is unnecessary, a compensation for the knowledge of one's own unimportance. But the soup and the bread and the healing and fixing and making were necessary. If she had not done them, someone else would have. Someone else would have to. But not as well or as kindly.

She cannot make the bread, now, and she can only stir the soup, and the only one who needs healing is her. She cannot fix what is wrong, cannot stuff the memories back into her head, cannot press her hands into the flesh of her children and remove knots from their shoulders and slivers from their fingers and sadness from their bellies. She cannot do things; she can only busy her hands, push the ring up and down her finger, push it and pull it and rub her finger smooth then wet then bleeding.

She cannot say things, either, only keep her mouth busy. She has few records left, and she spins them again and again—someone has said coffee, and so she tells the story of that time when my grandfather was at the coffee shop and I came to visit her and we surprised him there, oh wasn't that funny just to see the look on his face when we showed up at the coffee shop.

Someone has said dress, and so she tells the story of that time when she was shopping for dresses for the girls (and here we wonder if it was for my mother or me or my sister or all of us) with the money she saved so that they could have new dresses—it was important to have new dresses for special occasions; there is always enough for dresses when they are needed, she said.

(When she tells this story, though I am not sure of its subject, I feel again the embarrassment of things being purchased for me on a day that was neither my birthday nor Christmas.)

Someone has said shop and she is unsure, for a moment, whether this calls for the story of the coffee shop or the story of shopping for dresses for the little girls, and so she tells us of the time when she went to the coffee shop, only to find that it had closed and been replaced with a dress shop, so she bought dresses for the girls with some money she had saved for a special occasion.

She keeps her hands busy with the ring, and once it is removed, with the twisting of skin now too large for her body; she keeps her mouth busy with the same stories, told over and over again. She has nothing to do now—or nothing she is allowed to do—but she is busy all the same.

We put salve on her finger where the ring has rubbed it raw and bandage it tight against the air and the rubbing. It is too fat, with its bandage, for the ring to fit over top, and under the bandage her whole finger will turn white and wrinkled and soft.

She keeps her mind busy with stories, told at times when we have other things to discuss. And because she is not listening, because she interrupts with stories we have already heard, we look across the room at each other and smile knowingly (or perhaps unknowingly) and do not listen to her. We know the stories, after all, there is no need to tell them over again, with only the names different.

Don't worry, I whisper, when everyone else is gone. I will change the stories when I tell them. I will make a name that is not your name and it will be fall instead of spring outside the window. I will hide you behind my words (as I failed to before).

ঌ

We are in the kitchen.

It is noon, and I have been out with my grandfather for the morning, I think, playing with the dog on the farm or looking for turtles by the creek or learning to drive his truck down the road behind the woodshed, though I am too old to pretend the dog is a horse and too young to drive anything but a bicycle or a pony. My grandmother offers us a toasted cheese sandwich for lunch, she says she can do it in the oven or in the skillet on the stove, whichever I prefer.

I don't know, I say, just do whatever is easiest.

And my grandfather smiles and says, just do whatever is easiest, what a lovely girl we have here, grandmother, a girl who just wants you to do whatever is easiest, isn't that nice?

And she smiles, too, and says, isn't that

nice, but doesn't reach for the skillet or open the oven, she just stands there, with the loaf of bread in her hand, holding but not leaning on the counter, looking at me and smiling, with the pulled tooth just showing at the edge of her smile.

I have betrayed her, stupidly, foolishly, not knowing that choice is a humiliation. Whatever you want, I say, and I leave to wash up. Isn't that nice, my grandfather says, and he reaches up and grabs the skillet from the hook where my grandmother cannot reach without a stool and scoops a spoon of bacon fat from the tin on the stove and calls to me and says don't run off too far, the lunch will be ready soon.

🙠

It is a picture taken while you were looking somewhere else.

The tip of your nose is cut off by the edge

of the frame—you turned to look at my sister, I think, who is throwing popcorn in the air and catching it in her mouth, outside the part that we can see. You are laughing, and you have dropped the tissue that you are always carrying lately, though bits of it are still stuck to your fingers. Your hands are lifted up beside your face, surprised, catching the laughter that is spitting out like too-hot soup.

My grandfather is sitting beside you. His head is blurry because he is turning to look at you, and his arm has dropped from where it was holding you, in front of the camera. His skin is stretched too far, propped up like an old tent by the bones of his face.

I am not as young as I used to be, he would say if he were the one pasting this photo into your scrapbook. But he is not—I am the one pasting photos, and he is the one sitting beside you in the photograph, holding you for the camera.

My mother is the one taking the picture, her elbows propped on the table she is crouching behind. She waits one second too long—you have laughed, and my grandfather has turned, and my father's left arm has stepped into the background as he dabs some more paint onto his brush.

You are looking somewhere else in this next picture, too. My grandfather's arm is back around you, and a picture frame that caught the light in the last photograph has been turned down beneath the bottom edge of the picture.

My father has moved his brushes and his picture behind my mother, to be close to the window.

The sun has come out between the first photograph and this one, and my sister has finished her bowl of popcorn. You are looking over the top edge of the picture this time, and squinting with your whole face—my mother says it is because of the sun in your eyes.

I am standing behind my mother, waving at you from outside the picture, making faces at you that we both pretend no one else can see.

It is our little joke, I think in my head.

It is our little joke, you said to me—we will not tell your mother.

Or even my grandfather? I asked.

Or even him, you said. It is our little secret.

I am glad that we have found this secret on our first day together, I think (but do not tell you). Now we will have an entire week with a secret, and visits after that. When I come for Thanksgiving, I will make the sign with my fingers, and then you will laugh with me, and no one else will know why. I see now that this is how it goes: before the secret truths, there are the sideways smiles and shared, small lies.

This is our secret, you said.

☙

It is still there, underneath the piles of clothes and boxes of old canning jars. It is not gone, it is only hidden. Only hidden, just waiting for us to find it again. So see, let's look at these pictures, that is you in the photograph. And that is me beside you. Here we are, drawing pictures of owls in the morning. We are on Vacation together.

(I do not reveal that I used to think of Vacation as an island, or a country, or a footstool, something—regardless of its shape—with a definite border, something that one could be on. I do not reveal that going to a place not called Vacation seemed dishonest. I do not remind her that she knows of my former foolishness, that she is the one who explained Vacation to me while we sat drawing owls in the morning.)

That is me in the photographs, but younger. I am shouting at her in my head, but in the living room, on the couch in the afternoon, I am just talking. In my head I am saying re-member remember rememberre-memberre-memberre! but in the living room I am telling a story about how she taught me how to draw, how she sat with me while my sister cried, even when she was past the age of crying and I was not yet at the age where sitting with me was anything better than a task.

That is me in the photograph, but younger, she says, when I pause in my story to wrap a blanket around myself. I do not know who the—and here she points at herself—who that is, but that—and here she points at me—is me, only younger. My hair used to be the colour of yours, she said. And so she starts telling a story, but a different one than is in the photograph.

I did not have a grandmother for as many years as you, she said. Memories were not as long, then, as they are now, and so people died sooner. Their memories ran out, and they could not remember how to live, so they died. But when I was younger, when I was younger my grandmother was not dead. I think that might be her, in the picture. Yes, I think that is her. See how she looks like me, only older? See how we both have small hands?

She was teaching me to write my name, in this picture.

And, I ask her, and?

She was teaching me to write my name in this picture.

And what else? I ask (and what else, what else, what else, what else? I am asking inside). How old were you?

She was teaching me to write my name. See, I can still write my name now. There are some things worth remembering, she said, there are some things you shouldn't forget.

I nod and say mmm hmmm mmm hmmm.

And while I am nodding and mmm hmmm-ing, while I am looking across the room to the clock which I cannot read from this far away, she takes out a pen, or a marker, from one of those folds in a grandmother's sweater that always seems to contain something, an object invisible until it is procured at just the right time. And she signs her name. The two swooping loops of the capital letters perfectly framing my face and her face in the photograph.

Do you want to learn how to write your name, she asks.

ꕥ

This memory
is inscribed
on a piece of
bread in the
kitchen cupboard.
She left it there
on the shelf
two days ago
after lunch
forgetting that

Bread left out will stale.

This memory
is written
on the piece of
paper by
the telephone.
She left it there
by the phone
three days ago,

at dinner,
forgetting that

She cannot read it anymore.

This memory
is mixed in
with the batter
for pancakes
on the counter.
She dropped it there
in the milk

And stirred until smooth.

(This memory
is shaped like
the hole in the
centre of
your heart. Have you
forgotten that already?)

❧

At first, with care. A minutes-long infinity spent on a single shoelace.

I was not there to remember these early, deliberate memories. I see them only in hindsight, compressing shoelaces and the eternal rising of the first batch of bread and the chocolate birthday cake for a sister now dead or moved away into a single, sunny, everlasting afternoon.

I saw only the end of the second age, the careless, casual, immodest skills—bread left to rise while the roast was prepared, set to bake while she mended skirts and listened, patiently, to accounts of the creek in the woods told first by children and then by their children.

And I attended the whole of the third age. Memories deliberate, again, the cookbooks consulted, first furtively, and then without pretence of wisdom, or even knowledge. Memories whose use depleted the storehouse instead of reinforcing its walls. She rationed them, first fearful of losing a skill and then fearful of the discovery of loss.

❧

Tea that tastes like wet leaves:
stewed
and cooled
And strained to see
what you were doing
over the wires—flickering
and flashing
And blinking as you fell asleep
and pretended not to:
the game of tired children
who must stay awake
And alert us that you were coming,
he thought,
on the train (but perhaps on the bus)—

you had left a note
saying that you were coming for tea.

(He does not know the note is from six years ago, from the day you first suspected you were losing your mind. He does not know that you have filed your notes since then alphabetically, according to subject, and that now you re-use the best ones to hide your writing, which slants down and falls off the edge of the page. He does not know that, if he looks on the back of your note tomorrow, he will see a flyer from four years ago for the freezer that now sits in your basement, humming. He does not know that you will soon lose your box of notes, fallen behind their shelf into a hole between the floor and the wall that you did not know was there. He does not know that you gave away the last jar of pickles in the spring of this year, and that you filled the other, already-empty, jars with pickles from the store and sealed them against his knowing. His back is too bad, so he cannot stoop and then stand up to get into the cellar where the jars of pickles from the store are hidden behind the infinite supply of green tomato chutney that you are sure will never be used, though you keep it anyway. He only knows that you are leaving to go for tea and that you have given far more than you can spare of your memories away—quilts and dresses and jars of peaches and pickles and tatted tablecloths and letters written to grown-up children who wish now that they had saved them.)

I am not as young as I used to be, he says, smiling. But he does not know that you are no longer as young as he is, that while his age walks forward, back bent and head up, yours is rolling down the hill, a barrel not quite perfectly round, bumping but still going faster.

We know (or we knew) how to make the

bread without a recipe, and the soup that tastes like Sunday. We know that you like to come for tea, that you like it warm instead of hot (with more milk than tea) and that you like sugar to hide the bitterness of leaves steeped too long. I know about your box of notes, and the pickles from the store, which I saw when you sent me downstairs to get something that only I am tall enough to reach any more.

(He does not know that you once wanted to be a nurse. I did not know either, I only found out when my mother told me because she was sure you had forgotten.)

❧

A lot of my sentences have ended, lately, with this: we had the same conversation again, later.

A lot of hers have started with this: before I was old, before your mother left, before this happened, before your father fell, before the year of the green tomatoes, before the time when I couldn't remember, before, before, before.

Before your mother left, your grandfather never cooked, she said. He likes to cook now, he always likes to cook, he is always making me things, even when we go out to friends' for dinner, she says. I just have to sit with my feet up in my chair beside the fire. It is nice work if you can get it.

She forgets that between the time that my mother left and the time when my grandfather started to cook there were several years and several grandchildren, there was soup and the year with the green tomatoes, there was the bread that she made on the day I was born, there were pickles pushed under the brine by a jar of last year's preserves.

My grandfather bought the bread, unsliced, from the bakery across town, took it out of its paper bakery bag, and wrapped it in the big soft tea towels from the bottom of the drawer, tying them together across the loaf. Not as elegant, perhaps, as my grandmother's knots used to be, but her fingers now were not quite as nimble as they used to be, either. I'm not as young as I used to be, she would say, laughing, and the others would laugh along with her. Nor are we, nor am I, nor is she, they will say. We are not as young as we used to be, although you—and here they would point at my grandmother—you are certainly much younger than most. And they would laugh again. She would laugh too, thinking, perhaps, of the bakery bag, which her husband had carefully buried in the garbage, under cherry pits and pea pods and corn husks, before they left with their loaf to dinner. Is that a new recipe, they would ask? It is a little softer than I remember. Oh say, she would say, oh say! you know I don't use recipes. Bread is just made from,

from,

from...

She would trail off and laugh, and they would laugh with her again—oh you are sly, you can't be sharing your secrets, can you? Good bread is not as common as it used to be.

Before I was old I was young. I am not as young as I used to be, she would say, but I was young.

I know, I know, we are all not as young as we used to be.

But you are still young, she would say to me, as young as I used to be. Have you had your supper yet? Let me make you some dinner, we have ham left over from Sunday, I can make you a ham sandwich for lunch, would you like a ham sandwich? I always find a ham sandwich is good for breakfast with a piece of fruit.

Perhaps they always had ham, or perhaps she just liked ham the best of all. But every day she would offer me a ham sandwich, ham left over from Sunday. And perhaps a ham sandwich was just a word for something else, something that she had forgotten; maybe ham sandwich sounded like something she remembered (or something she would like to remember). But every day she would offer me a ham sandwich, for breakfast or lunch or for supper.

I am not as young as I used to be, but I can still make you a ham sandwich. You come up and visit sometime, and we will have ham sandwiches—they are your favourite, aren't they?

We had this same conversation again, later—and again, after that.

Before the year with the green tomatoes, you didn't even know what green tomatoes were, did you? she continues. You didn't know that we could eat them in mince-meats and chutneys and that I hid them in spaghetti sauce when you weren't looking. Oooh, I would laugh when I knew that you were eating them and you didn't know...you didn't know that you were eating green tomatoes...you thought...you thought...

Before that happened I could trust him, or I thought I could trust him. Her voice has changed, suddenly; it has sharpened, as if there is no relation between her and the person speaking a moment ago. (It happens often now, this changing into a new person. The book I was reading said to expect it, but expected tragedies are often harder to bear than unexpected ones.) Before that I could trust him.

(She is referring, I know, to the day that she mixed up the salt and the sugar—both in glass jars in the cupboard—and killed the yeast and still did not know her mistake and so made an entire batch of sweet rolls with the sugarsalt and the saltsugar, and fed them to us and watched, confused, as we gagged.)

He can't be trusted any more, she said, furtively, looking into my eyes like the men on the corner with the magazines who try to stop me on my way home from the market. He can't be trusted any more, he takes things away. He is not as nice as he used to—

And just as suddenly she stops, switches back, and is reminiscing again—I am not as young as I used to be!

You have forgotten, haven't you, she continues, (in a different voice again) that you used to breathe through your belly, the seat of your soul, that there were holes in your heart for breathing that did not close until you had nearly forgotten they were there.

(I pretend to listen, make believe that I understand what she is saying.)

If you had not forgotten, at the moment of your birth, all that had gone before, you would have died, rather than continue.

(Before I was born, I breathed through my stomach, through holes in my heart, I repeated.)

They are sealed now against memory (though mine is breaking open), pressed and closed so that we can remember our past. When they break, we remember another past, an older one. The time before birth is preserved in brine, corroding and waiting until at last it makes a hole and leaks out to dissolve the present.

(Wait, wait, I want to say. I am listening

now, can you repeat that? But of course she cannot, and I do not bother to ask. Instead I back out of her room slowly, as she mutters at me, or at the wall.)

Salt is preserver, salt is destroyer; salt corrodes, salt preserves. Eating the bottoms of cars and drawing out water from bacon and crusting the edges of pants dragged along the ground in winter.

ℒ

There had been a word, once, for the moment between waking and dreaming, for the crescent dinner rolls spread inside with butter. There had been a word for the patterns of dead leaves stained onto concrete sidewalks, for the impressions of fall left over into spring. There had been a word for the memories of dreams.

They are dissolved now, I suppose, sloshing around inside of you—words that once circumscribed flesh, now bound up inside it and broken.

We tried to name them again, you and I. We wanted to name them so that no one could forget, so they could not disappear.

But the names stuck to our tongues. We tried to spit them out; we pressed our tongues to the roofs of our mouths, rubbed them along the ridge of our teeth, scratched the back of our throats to make a smooth road for the words to slide out. And still they stuck to our tongues, inside us instead of around us.

You opened the door to let in the cool of the night, but you did not know that you would let the night in as well, that the coolness could not come without darkness.

❧

You cannot tell someone with no past to remember. She will only mistake her invention for memory and send you all into town when you meant to go sit in the park.

She did not remember yesterday, or the day before. She does not remember getting dressed, and so she pulls on slacks over her skirt, and sweaters she may once have knitted over blouses and undershirts. She does not remember eating, and so she reaches for the box of stale crackers, before she forgets again what to do with them in her hands.

She does not remember that tomorrow is her birthday, that all of the bright paper squares, folded and set up in the window, are hers. That tomorrow she is leaving for a while.

She has no past, anymore, so she has made one for herself, as girls make stories for their dolls. She points to herself in the mirror by the door, before we go to the park: you are looking awfully nice today, she says. Do you want to go to the park? Me and my friends are going! And she gestures over her shoulder to the mirror behind her, across from the one she is gazing into; she smiles, coy and slightly cross-eyed, at the smaller and smaller selves receding into the space behind the mirror.

We go to the park often. There was a nice boy there, a nice boy, too bad...he was such a nice boy. This is the park where I met your grandfather, she says to my mother (though I think she means to speak to me). What a nice boy, he was such a nice boy. We were dancing in the kitchen to one of his mother's records, that boy sure couldn't dance, what a nice boy...she trails off like this often, smiling and ending with words that didn't mean anything, even when she understood them. A nice boy, Oh say! It was interesting, Funny how that happens, Well that was a different day, then—She isn't as young as she used to be.

We have been to the park many times. It is a lovely park, there is a piece at the back where the people from...from...(here she flaps her hands, trying to mean the people from the stitched-together houses without grass in the front), where they can grow vegetables. She tries to smile, but the effort of holding both compassion and condescension in her mouth is too much, and it comes out as a grimace instead.

Do you want to go to the park? she says, noticing me. Her hand flaps again, like she is petting a dog this time. I met your father at the park, she says, still looking at me (though I think she means to speak to my mother). What a nice boy, he was such a nice boy. Did you know that he proposed before he had even met my father? That sort of thing wasn't done in those days, you know. He said I'm going to marry you, if it's the last thing I do! Doesn't sound much like a proposal, does it, but your father always knew what he wanted, and I wanted the same thing.

Let's go to the park, what are you waiting for? She's impatient now, stomping and flapping, and we should have switched her shoes onto the right feet while she was distracted by her stories. What are you waiting for, girls, we've got to get going, we've got to get going, your father's coming home before you know it, we've got to get going. I am confused, looking to my mother for direction, but she is looking back at me, and I realize that we must look very like the two sisters that my grandmother is mistaking us for. It's okay, I say, it's okay, we're ready to go. We've got your jacket, we're ready to go.

The three of us troop out the door to the park, my grandmother still telling us we've got to get going, though her voice is quieter once we're outside. We turn the corner and now she is telling another story, this one about a man from the train company who called for your grandfather—oh sure you are, I said, and I'm the Prime Minister! Your father even smiled at that one—

The park is that way, she interrupts herself, tugging on my mother's arm. Why aren't we going to the park? We turn left at the brick house, and left again at the wooden one, that's how we get to the park. I remember, that's how we get to the park. If we turn right here, we will come to the end of the street, not to the park. I used to go there all the time, she says, with an authority known only to children and the very wise, we don't turn right here. (But we do, I think, she must remember that we turn right here—left leads into town, surely she knows that, surely she is just mistaken.)

I look at my mother, both of us making up reasons to make her reasonable.

It's getting dark—

The sun's too bright—

We say at once, and start to laugh, pitying ourselves and our lies and this strange woman who knows that we must turn left.

You're right, I say, and my mother nods; we do turn left here to get to the park, but why not go right, and you can tell us about the neighbourhood there?

Why not, echoes my mother?

Why not, says my grandmother, and we turn to the right, towards the park, through the past and into this present, imperfect and beautiful.

❧

Will you read to me?

It is not the first time she has asked, in a voice that reminds me too much of my own, many years ago.

Will you read me a story?

I cannot refuse her; I understand now why she never refused me.

This one, this one, read this one.

Her words are slower than mine must have been, but firmer, too—they have had longer to set.

This one, read this one.

She is pushing an unfamiliar volume towards me.

This one, read this one.

I take it from her and unwind the string holding the leaves together. The writing inside the cover is familiar. It is her diary. Her life's story, from before writing such things was fashionable.

Will you read to me?

(Does she know which book she has picked? Does part of her know and not the other part, the left hand blind to the right?) Not today, I say, wincing, maybe tomorrow? Maybe a different one today?

It is harder to lie to those who used to lie to you, who once knew the difference between lies and truths and stories, but for whom everything now is true. It is easier, I imagine, to lie to those who will one day understand your lies, who will grow up to justify them for you. But I am lying to someone who will never grow up.

No, this one. Read this one.

I am embarrassed for her, though she can no longer feel shame. Why should I be embarrassed, ashamed for this woman who can know neither why she has chosen this book nor why I am refusing her? She will not notice if I open it and tell another story, if I skip the pages that are too intimate to read.

Today was sunnier than I expected—

This one, read this one.

I am reading this one, I shout in my head. I am reading this one, or I am pretending to, which should be the same thing to you.

Today was sunny, sunnier than yesterday. The girls came over—

This one, read this one.

It was sunny today—

This one, read this one.

I wonder if she notices that the story changes each time I start it. I wonder if she remembers what she has written, if she is trying to make me understand, if I am actually supposed to read aloud these tiny sheaves full of children unexpected and a husband away, of pages-long exposition followed by days described only as sunny; cloudy; overcast, but it did not rain. There is nothing in here of bread or preserves, of the things I thought days were made of.

You are not the person I wish to remember! I yell at the grandmother (barely even a mother, yet) of the diary; I yell silently, of course, so as not to interrupt the reading.

This one.

She is pointing now, and her words are even slower.

This one.

She is falling asleep, I only need to pretend for a moment longer.

It was sunny today, sunnier than usual. The baby slept through the night, and I took her outside to plant. We will put up some asparagus tomorrow, and maybe some strawberry jam...

❧

If this is the end, then we must not be caught waiting, I hear someone say, as if we knew and expected and were only hanging around until the knowledge became flesh. It must come as if we had never expected it. Pretend that you do not know, that you are not waiting to take the last spoonful of soup, pretend that you do not want to believe in each minute as a possible infinity of tiny divisions.

(And I know you will say you have not thought such things. I know you will act as if you just forgot the last bite of soup, as if you were not believing to yourself that the dribble still left was keeping your hands warm and keeping the end from coming.)

But an empty bowl, or a near-empty bowl, no more saves you than it warms your hands. And an infinite minute is a lie of calculus, a graph repurposed as comfort. She is dying (or already dead, some might say) and you are dying, and everything around you—the soup moulding in the fridge, the pickles improperly sealed, the bread with its heels and top sliced off in a paper bag on the table—is dying or dead. The peonies outside the window are growing on the death of tulips and already they are dying; they will be planted over with chrysanthemums in the fall.

She is dying, and you are waiting, though you lie to me and say you are not.

If everything is dying, then it is easily possible to forget that particular things must have their own moment to die. It is simple to believe that one single death could be unexpected. So go on about your own dying, do not be caught waiting, as if waiting could stop the thing from happening.

Your words cannot save her, continued my mother, only remind you of what was before.

There are always endings, just as there are always beginnings—both there for those who know (or care) to look. But it would be just as true, she said, to say that there are never endings or beginnings, that what you think is the end is really just the waiting place before you stumble over the horizon. And what you thought was the start of the story is only the place where you came in.

There are always endings, she said. They are all cut off, severed, some more elegantly than others, some tapered so expertly that they pass away unnoticed. You do not write to the end (as I know you wish to do), you do not walk up to the horizon and finish. There is no place where the horizon ends, only places you cannot yet see.

ꟗ

People should live longer than their food.

My grandmother died last week. She left her jewellery to my younger sister, her house to my aunt and uncle and their children, and most of the rest of her possessions to the secondhand shop where she volunteered the first and second Tuesday of the month. She left me her food.

When I was younger, when we cooked together, I would stand on a stool, barely able to get my shoulders above the countertop. Before she died, she would stand on a stool and still barely reach up to my shoulders. It was understood between us, just after I made my first turkey, that lessons had been discontinued and I was grown up now—she knew this even when I did not—and we were no longer so close in age as we once had been. I had outgrown the stool as she grew into it, and had copied out her instructions when she could not. None of these things meant I had grown up, but the first turkey decided that I was now too old to be privy to the secrets she told, though still too young to tell them myself.

By the time she died, we had not cooked together for a year. I was surprised, then, that she left me her food. She had already been gone from the house for days before she died, I didn't even know if there would be any unspoiled food left.

I went through the cupboards and the pantry, touching their careful labels that acted as a bulwark against forgetfulness. The pantry was mostly bare—lately she'd abandoned dry goods and ate only fresh things from the market. The cupboards were similarly emptied by inattentiveness, and on the second day of my cleaning and sorting, several of the volunteers from the secondhand shop came in and then left with her dishes and glasses. Only the serviette and teaspoon cupboard looked as it had.

The vegetables in the fridge had rotted by the time I got there. Sweet potatoes sat on the counter and two acorn squash acted as a centrepiece in a wicker basket that used to belong to my great-aunt.

I left her house after the third day, carrying the squash, the yams, and the dregs of the pantry. I had already taken her tea supply to the house of her best friend as an offering for the wake. I thought of freeze-drying the yams, or hollowing out the squash and making rattles, but instead I made a soup and topped it with stale saltines from the pantry.

I had never been willed food before, I wasn't sure what the protocol was.

My sister called me three weeks after the funeral. It was the first we'd spoken since the funeral; she was away, visiting a friend newly married. She asked if I had checked the cellar.

I went in to work early the next day so as to take a long lunch, and drove the half-hour to my grandmother's house. Someone was there with a key from my aunt, measuring the spare room for bunk beds and two desks.

I went downstairs to the cellar. Food was arranged by year and then alphabetically, except three years ago's preserves, which were overwhelmed by the green tomatoes that my grandmother had tried to save from the frost with a combination of chutney, mincemeat, and an unsuccessful attempt at jelly.

I was much younger the last time that green tomatoes were plentiful, old enough to know what bread was but not yet old enough to make it on my own. I stayed at my grandmother's house overnight, in the bed that ceased to be my aunt's when she went away, and we made pizza. My grandmother made buns, actually, but she gave me a piece of the dough to do with what I wanted. She had hidden the green tomatoes in a sauce made of ripened ones, and I used that for my pizza; I grated cheese into a little aluminum tray and then sprinkled it on. I ate the buns that my grandmother made, and wrapped the pizza in already-used foil and took it home. I cut it into four pieces, one for each of my mother, sister, father, and me.

I made it to eat together, in the same way that the first pieces of a chocolate cake cannot be eaten alone.

My mother came home, after I was in bed, and ate a slice of it as a snack.

It was so delicious, she said later, but then

there were only three slices left; I hadn't taken fractions yet, and I didn't know about dividing three pieces into four parts. So it stayed in the freezer, frost growing like mould on the piece of masking tape that I used to hold the foil together, until my mother cleaned it out. My mother is a great believer in cleaning things out.

I have forgiven my mother for much greater things than pizza. But small things escape, like the crumbs that stay in the corner because the bristles of the broom are too wide to notice them.

Last year's canning had labels on the bottoms of the jars. They were all inscribed with my name.

For the rest of that fall, I ate only my grandmother's food. Pickled sausages and concentrated grape juice, dilled asparagus and peaches with cinnamon and cloves. I ate straight from the jars, and cleaned and stacked the empty ones in front of my kitchen window, each jar catching and releasing sun at new angles.

I got sick on green tomato mincemeat for breakfast.

I left work early every Tuesday to eat pickled garlic cloves at four o'clock, as we used to when my grandmother would get home from the secondhand store just as I was arriving at her house after school.

I finished a few weeks before Christmas. The days were short enough that I could no longer tell what kinds of patterns the glasses were making in the window, because I left and came back in the dark. I sometimes feared that December light was like trees falling in a forest, and that I should leave work earlier or go in later in order to see it and reassure it of existence.

I missed eating things that were dry.

I began to crave the bread that my grandmother and I had baked when I was younger.

I looked for a recipe, but could not find one.

⁂

The ending was not as I had pictured.

It was at first exactly as I had imagined, with the smell of bread finally replacing the smell of yeast, and the tops of the loaves hard when I knocked on them with my middle knuckle, the one that feels nothing but the perfect doneness of bread. There were spaces inside for the butter to melt in, and each loaf clung to the bottom of the pan for a moment before it fell onto the counter to cool. They are done! I would say, We are done!

We must wash the bowl, put the pans away, and make the rest of dinner, my grandmother said. It is not made from talking, or from watching.

My sister would come in and cut off the heel of the bread, spread it with the last of the butter, and take it onto the porch, where she sat, reading, on the wicker chair until dinner was ready. She took one of the loaves to the neighbours' house, to thank them for the jelly of earlier that week. We filled the sink with water and began washing the bowl.

It could have stayed in the oven for a minute longer; I see now that the top was not quite as brown as I would have liked. We didn't need to wash the dishes right away, there was still time before my grandfather came in from the yard for dinner.

We could have waited once it was done, left the oven open, let the smell stay for a minute longer before replacing it with lemon dish soap.

But there were dishes to do, then, and now there are flowers to press and condolences to write and jars to wash for next year's peaches. And nothing will live in the jars this winter, unless you count the spiders, and my oven at home is not big enough to make a whole batch of bread.

For a moment, it seemed she was ready to die. But now I realize that I was not yet as wise as I had wished, and that the flowers outside the window would have opened wider tomorrow.

So now today,
when you can only see
me with your hands,
and can only hear me
in your echoes,
is the moment you pick
to tell me that

you now live in the space
between hearing
and heard. (Or two other
such things, that, like
us, it makes no sense to separate.)

&

It was easier, I see now, to write instead of visit; I did not even need to seek absolution for my neglect, because today is a new day, the first day, and she is meeting me for the first time.

It is forgetting as redemption.

&

It is winter again, and I am always cold.

I would like to remember what it is to be neither cold nor warm, to be unaware of myself. But I only remember now and the hot summer, the feeling of never being warm and of always being hot. I seem to have forgotten the spring and fall that I am sure have passed and will come again.

(That is not entirely true.)

I am not always cold; I remember what it is to be warm enough, which is not the same as being warm. I remember the feeling of falling asleep with my pyjamas tucked into my socks, so that the space between my ankles and my calves did not get cold and wake me.

You know what they say—cold hands, warm heart! my grandmother would say as she rubbed my hands between hers.

But what about cold feet? I would ask.

Cold feet, eat more meat!

Cold feet, morning brings sleet!

Cold feet, when can we meet?

She took my feet in her hands and rubbed them, too.

Her skin felt insubstantial though her hands were strong—meat filling barely contained by layers of papery pastry spread with butter. She was not always cold, though her daughter and granddaughter were. Her hands were always warm, fresh from the oven.

☙

This is how I waited
for you to die.
This is how I waited
when you were sick
(and before you were sick)
when I realized you were old
(or at least smelled old).
(You used to smell like rose soap.)
We all smell like old men in our sleep
(but now you smell like old men when you're waking).

Can you die in the middle of a sentence, or do you sense it coming on and finish up the sentence before it is your turn to go? (And here we are talking of dying from old age, or from some disease that long ago told you it would last as long as you did, not from swords or guns or the sudden, mysterious falling over while cooking or planting or going to the store.) Or do you try to finish but hurry forward too fast, stumbling off the edge of the page?

I am waiting for you to die, though I pretend otherwise.

Before I was waiting we were resting together. We sat down, briefly, between the end of the horizon and the beginning of tomorrow, catching our breath and our souls, which had threatened to fall behind our bodies.

But after they had caught up, we were still sitting, still resting, until resting turned, I am not sure how, into waiting, though we did not know for what. There was nothing to indicate the change, though we knew it had happened (just as there was nothing to tell us that you were not merely growing old, any more, that keys in the fridge and shoes in the pantry were now things to cry over instead of laugh about).

&

The last thing she forgot was how to speak; her words left with the closing of the day. They left in the midst of the description of loss, until there was nothing left upon which to inscribe the memory of forgetting.

&

(She was not wise
as I have pretended.
She did not speak
as a poet ought to,
or make Meanings
out of pomegranates.
She spoke in words,
not in Metaphors or
Similes, like

she should have, or, rather
as I wanted her to.
What is art, then,
but the preparations
for our supper?)

ꟹ

How do you describe the time after words?

Mouths open and empty, words pushed in and dribbled out again, teeth (or the memories of teeth) closing over the space left behind.

There is no space for you here anymore, so breathe out and do not breathe in again, someone else will do it for you. Hold this in your mouth until it dissolves, you do not need to swallow, someone else will do that for you. You do not need this anymore, so stop looking, it will only tire you out. Someone else can do that for you. We will pack up the boxes and line them with tissue, paste labels onto them so that you can tell them apart.

ꕥ

To remember is to make again, you told me once. So I will make your favourite things, the bread and the sweet pickles, and I will buy the flowers from the store that you used to grow in pots beside the door.

It is no memory if you do not make it yourself, you also said, though I pretend to forget that part.

I will take the pictures from their frames and bring them to the photographer's house, I will ask him if he can make them larger, easier to see, because your eyes are not so good, anymore, and it is hard for you to tell the difference between your sisters in the picture of you all at the beach.

These are not memories, you would tell me, if you could speak in words I understood.

These are only reminders, though I am not
sure what they are reminders of—

—but I thank you all the same, I imagine
you saying, and you touch my arm as you ask
me to cut up the pickles into small pieces
and soak the bread in some milk in that dish.
Perhaps you could stay a little longer?

Credits

I first must thank Dr. Nina Kolesnikoff, who was bold in encouraging me to begin this book and kind in her comments throughout the process. Her confidence in me and my writing is much greater than I deserve. Dr. Kathy Garay has also been with this manuscript since before the beginning. Though the right words often felt beyond my grasp, she was ever-confident in urging me to find them.

Kerry Scott—editor, confidante, and friend—was the midwife of this book. Though it may have gotten finished without her, it certainly would not have finished as well, or as wonderfully.

I have had many remarkable teachers, among them Mrs. Janie Senko-Driedger, grade one teacher extraordinaire and laminator of my first "published" book; Mrs. Maxine Vakaras, who told me when I could do better; Ms Nora Martin, who taught me more about good writing than anyone before or since; and Mrs. Kim Corvino, who created a space for that writing to flourish.

Few children grow up with all four grandparents, and even fewer live close enough to go to baseball games and make zwieback and have sleepovers with regularity. My four remarkable grandparents—Marion and Bert Abbott, John and Mary Wiebe—are the ones that other children dream of having, but that I actually get to have.

Finding a publisher was supposed to be the hardest part, but meeting Patrick Boyer was actually quite easy and delightful. Along with Dominic Farrell and Gary Long, he has made the experience of publication even lovelier than expected.

My mom, sister, and dad have always encouraged my aspirations, even though they were often different than everyone else's. Mom and Hilary in particular have been alongside me during challenges even greater than this one, and their acts of love always seem to come at just the right time.

Finally, I would like to invent a word much larger than thank-you for my husband Tim, who has not yet known me apart from the writing of this book. Though it often consumed me, he stayed and loved me anyway.

CATHERINE M.A. WIEBE was born in the town of Simcoe, Ontario, and now lives, writes, and tries to recreate her grandmothers' food in Hamilton. She is a recent graduate of the Arts and Science Program at McMaster University, and has been writing (with a few other jobs on the side) since before her graduation. She is married to Tim, and they live in a little brick cottage with a yellow door and a fledgling garden outside.

Interview with the Author

Several reviewers say your prose reads like poetry. How do you describe your writing style?

CATHERINE M.A. WIEBE: As that of someone who cares desperately for meaning, and Truth, and beauty, and wants to find words that express that care.

So do you see Second Rising *as a poem? Is there a difference, for you, between poetry and fiction?*

WIEBE: Yes, there is a difference between poetry and fiction, though I think of it as more of a membrane than a wall. I'd say *Second Rising* moves about the membrane.

You begin the book with a number of questions. Is that how you began the writing of the book, with questions?

WIEBE: Definitely. Though I wouldn't say that I ended it with answers...

You paint the connection between a grandmother and granddaughter in some truly remarkable scenes in Second Rising. *What, at its essence, is this special bond that bridges across generations?*

WIEBE: The very old and the very young are much closer in age, I think, than those of us in between.

You are a young writer, yet Second Rising *has a decidedly elegiac tone. That is largely due to the advancing illness of the grandmother but there seems to be a more general nostalgia as well. Do you have a particular attraction to the past?*

WIEBE: Not so much to the past as to the preservation of things passing away.

Did you plan to write a book from an early age?

WIEBE: I've wanted to write since I was six or seven, but the desire became a plan when I was in university.

How has your work editing other people's writing and doing graphic layout for publications influenced your own approach to creative writing, if at all?

WIEBE: Removing the specks from others' writing makes me keenly aware of the planks in my own.

The way humans first learn about things and then remember them is something you pay a lot of attention to in this book. What particular insight or experience caused your intense interest in memory?

WIEBE: Not one particular experience so much as a constellation of them—witnessing others' memory loss, watching children learn to think and remember, and a desire to make sense and beauty from things both intangible and important.

Sometimes quite startling in Second Rising *is the presentation of food and representation of edible things. What quality about food makes you see it as more than just something nutritious?*

WIEBE: We are very good at forgetting, and food's presence—as both symbol and sustenance—within our intimate rituals and traditions makes it into something that nourishes our memories as well as our bodies.

Your book's title comes from a step in the process of making bread. Can you explain what a "second rising" is in the making of bread and why you decided to use this term as a title?

WIEBE: The second rising is typically the rising that takes place after the bread has been shaped into loaves or rolls, just before it is placed in the oven. It is the rising when things begin to take their final shape, though that shape is still fragile…

Among the many things your book celebrates, the joy of working, of doing things with one's hands, stands out, if only because so much of modern life seems to involve trying to avoid doing such work. Yet the baking of bread, the laying down of preserves, the mending of clothes, is actually celebrated in your book. Why do you think such things are important?

WIEBE: Physical tasks and rituals are never only themselves—they connect us to each other and to truths that are important to remember in ways that mental exertion alone cannot. There is something more in almost every task we do, particularly the ordinary ones, and it is this moreness, this richness, that I hope to remind others of.

In writing this story for a society where Alzheimer's disease and memory loss seem to be affecting more people, do you hope to introduce a fresh cultural perspective to how memory works?

WIEBE: Alzheimer's and dementia more generally were both on my mind as I wrote. The beauty of loss, rather than just its sadness, is something I wish we cherished and celebrated more.

The remembrance of things past and lost is a celebrated literary theme, although you seem to reverse that by looking at what happens when the object remains but there is no one left to hold its memory. Should we be reading your book as an exploration of metaphysics?

WIEBE: Yes—in the broad sense of being concerned with more than is physically apparent.

You write in your book, "Memory will sustain you." Is Second Rising *an attempt to preserve memories, or is it a created memory? Do you think that created memories can be as sustaining as true ones?*

WIEBE: Yes, yes, and yes. Preservation and re-creation are often inseparable, and both "true" and "created" memories can be sustaining—though what, exactly, each sustains is another matter.

Second Rising *looks at impending death, yet there is no mention made of spiritual matters—or at least not religious matters. I wondered if the title,* Second Rising, *had any kind of a religious overtone, at least in relation to the book.*

WIEBE: The spiritual need not be mentioned in order to be present; I didn't intend a specifically religious meaning when choosing the title, but I would not dismiss such an interpretation.

Finally, what satisfied you most in writing Second Rising?

WIEBE: The feeling, at the end of it all, that I had written something of value.

Protecting the Environment

The text paper in this book, Rolland Enviro 100 from Cascades, is EcoLogo™ and Forest Stewardship Council certified. Containing 100 per cent post-consumer recycled fibre, it was processed chlorine free and manufactured with energy from biogas recovered from a municipal landfill site and piped to the mill.

The cover stock, Mohawk Via Felt from Mohawk Fine Papers, contains 30 per cent post-consumer recycled fibre. All of the electricity used to manufacture it was offset with certified wind-power certificates.